UNDER HER SKIN

Visit us at www.boldstrokesbooks.com

By the Author

Amigas y Amor Series

Little White Lie

Under Her Skin

To Sue —
I read from Picture
Imperfect just for you!

Under Her Skin

xo
Lea
Santos

by

Lea Santos

2010

UNDER HER SKIN

ISBN 10: 1-60282-162-3
ISBN 13: 978-1-60282-162-0

This Trade Paperback Original Is Published By
Bold Strokes Books, Inc.
P.O. Box 249
Valley Falls, NY 12185

First Edition: August 2010

Credits
Editor: Stacia Seaman
Production Design: Stacia Seaman
Cover Design By Sheri (graphicartist2020@hotmail.com)

Acknowledgments

Thank you to the BSB family. Thank you to my family, both genetic and chosen. Most of all, thank you to the family of readers who support lesbian fiction so fervently. You all totally rock.

Dedication

To my abuelo, Eusebio, and my sweet abuelita, Amada, for showing me every day that everyone—regardless of race, ethnicity, appearance, religion, socioeconomic status, weird grooming habits, or a penchant for drinking OJ straight from the carton—is worthy of love. And to my amazing, exasperating, brilliant dad. We butted heads like two stubborn rams, but thank you for trusting me to join the crew and be one of the "invisible Mexicans with the leaf blower" that college summer long ago (although the bikini probably didn't help with the invisibility factor, but hey, I was nineteen). Still, it's one of the best memories of you and me. Twenty-one years have flown by. I miss you.

CHAPTER ONE

Y ou have *got* to be kidding me." Dismay gripped Iris Lujan's stomach as tightly as she white-knuckled her BlackBerry. "Tonight?"

"It's short notice, sweetheart, but I just got word myself," said her longtime business manager, Geraline Moreno, as though completely disrupting Iris's schedule was the least of her worries. "It took artful maneuvering to work a Denver layover into Antoine's schedule." Geraline sniffed. "He's due here in Milan day after tomorrow. The least you can do is work with me."

Antoine, Schmantoine. Iris would rather shave her head shiny bald than spend the evening in the brain-melting company of Ego Boy. So what if he was the modeling world's newest designer underwear sensation. Every time she'd been around him, he'd acted like a shallow, conceited, Generation Millennial twit. It shamed her enough just knowing they shared the same career. Being seen in public with him? Over the top. "Can't he go alone?"

"You're better with the media."

"A potted plant is better with the media, Geraline. That's not my problem," she said in a peevish voice. "Why should I have to suffer because Antoine's a dumbass? I'm supposed to be on vacation, you know."

"I'm asking for one night."

"Vacation," she sang.

"One short evening. Is that too much to ask?"

"One *long, tedious* evening with the big blond womanizing egomaniac, just because he can't handle his own career where the media is concerned? Damn right it's too much to ask. I'm not a babysitter."

"I know, dear."

"You know, some models *should* just be photographed and remain silent."

"I know."

Iris massaged her temples. "Do you realize how long it has been since I've taken a real vacation?"

"I've been your manager for thirteen years, cupcake. Of course I know."

"Yeah, ever heard of a rhetorical question? And don't call me cupcake." She emitted a humorless huff and padded barefoot out onto the vast stone terrace overlooking Geraline's perfectly manicured gardens—Iris's favorite part of Gerri's Denver estate. The warm spring air swirled the ankle-length sundress around her calves.

"Look," Geraline said, in a conciliatory tone. "I know you don't particularly like Antoine—"

"He's a twenty-one-year-old, self-absorbed dumbass!"

"But once you get past the cameras at the restaurant opening, just avoid him, okay?"

Iris shook her head in dismay. "If you'll recall, Antoine is harder to shake than a smoking habit. And he continues to hit on me, Ger, even though he knows damn well I'm gay. That infuriates me. You know it does, and you said you would talk to him about it."

"Settle down, Iris. Like you said, he's twenty-one. And male. It's hormonal."

"Not my problem."

"Well, having a hot commodity like Antoine hit on you in public is good for your image."

"Ger, get it through your head. I don't *care* if people know I'm gay."

"You don't. But some of your big accounts may."

Iris scoffed. "Do they know what *year* it is, for God's sake?"

"Just smile and sparkle and do your thing, that's all I'm asking." Geraline paused, then turned on the charm. "There will be lots of media VIPs there. Where's that can-do attitude you've always had?"

Iris scowled. Gerri's schmoozing wouldn't cut it this time. "It went from can-do to did-too-much to don't-wanna-do-no-more, because I'm burned out. And, hey—check out this fresh concept—I'm on *va-ca-tion*. That's supposed to mean six whole weeks without working."

Gerri's long, put-upon sigh carried over the transcontinental phone lines, but she remained otherwise silent.

Uh-oh. Here it came, seeping in like groundwater through a poorly sealed basement. The big "G" began to slowly drown Iris's conscience, and she flailed. Guilt had always been her downfall, damned Catholic upbringing. Since Geraline was in Milan, she had generously invited Iris to spend her vacation at the Denver estate. This option simultaneously gave Iris the breathing space she needed to recharge, and allowed her to be near family and friends without the inconvenience of invading their guest rooms and disrupting their daily routines. She supposed she owed Geraline one stupid night, no matter how horrific she knew it would be. "Fine. If you're going to subject me to the silent treatment, I'll go. But I'm not happy about it."

"That's my girl." Geraline's triumphant smile oozed through every syllable, which only increased Iris's grumpiness. "I don't even mind if you sulk, sweet cheeks. Just look pretty while you do it."

Look pretty? Zing! The grumpiness meter shot off the scale. Iris clenched her jaw and wondered just how many times she'd heard that phrase pop out of Geraline's mouth over the years.

Thousands? Millions? "Gimme a break," she mumbled. Gerri's money-obsessed brain held Iris trapped in a gilded box. She was the visual package—period. Geraline expected nothing more of her. Understandable on one level, Iris supposed, since she was a model. But Gerri's constant assumptions about her superficiality irritated the shit out of Iris. Sheesh.

There were models like Antoine; *then* there was her.

Different animals.

"What's with you lately, kiddo?" Geraline seemed unduly solicitous all of a sudden, having won the battle of wills. "You used to be so enthusiastic about your job."

The subtle caring notes in Geraline's voice urged Iris to succumb. She didn't want to bear this mental burden alone anymore. She sank onto a chaise and pulled her shades off the top of her head onto the bridge of her nose. The late-afternoon sun glared over the jutted blue frame of the Rockies. She sighed. "I don't know. My heart's just not in it."

"Now, there's a news flash," Gerri said in a wry tone. "My question is why? Especially at this stage in your career."

Iris bristled at Gerri's flippant manner, not to mention the veiled insult. Her emotional drawbridge creaked back up, slammed closed. "Meaning I'm old?"

Geraline's hesitation gave Iris all the answer she needed. Still, Gerri added, "Well, we both know modeling years are like dog years, babe. You've got to admit, you're getting a little gray around the snout."

"Thanks a lot," Iris groused, irritated partly because she knew Geraline was right, but mostly because she'd almost been dumb enough to forget Gerri's relentless business agenda long enough to think, even for a split second, that spilling her guts to the woman would be a comfort.

Facts were facts, however. Iris had been modeling since the age of seventeen, and at thirty, she truly was edging over the hill, by industry standards. According to Geraline, Iris should be grateful for every contract she received.

Ironically, it was precisely her stage in life that made Iris feel so…unsettled. She had recently signed a new high-dollar but demanding print contract with Jolie Cosmetique, which started in six weeks. In Paris. It was a great assignment, one she would've celebrated landing only a couple of years ago. But she wasn't the only one aging; her parents had grown older, too. Did she really want to live so far away from them—and her friends—for the next three years? Alone?

Always alone.

Come to think of it, *that* was getting old, too.

After thirteen years, the fast-track, jet-setting lifestyle wasn't quite so fun anymore. She appreciated all the luck she'd had. Modeling—especially at the level she'd reached—had been extremely lucrative. It had secured her future and made her famous, and for that, she'd be forever grateful. But none of it— fame, money, world travel—mitigated the degradation of being treated like a piece of meat who should shut up and look pretty, or the sense of isolation that had begun to weigh heavily on her.

The last time she'd met with the heads of Jolie, they'd walked around her poking and prodding, talking about her in third person as if she were 110 pounds of horseflesh on the bidding block. She hated feeling less than human, yet that's exactly how this industry had begun to make her feel. That incident hadn't been the first.

"Did she put on a couple pounds?" the prospective clients would ask, directing their questions to anyone but her. "Her stomach looks poochy."

"Too ethnic. Will she go blond?"

"She's *ill*? Well, drug her up and get her over here. We've got a schedule to keep. Besides, the junkie look is red hot right now."

Blech. A seventeen-year-old ingénue might be able to tolerate such demeaning treatment, but it was slightly harder to stomach at thirty. She'd begun to feel like a sell-out, sacrificing who she was for what she did. Was it wrong that she yearned for a deeper purpose, for something to make her feel more…rooted? But how could she explain this soul-deep need to a businesswoman like Geraline, for whom success was measured in designer labels and dollar signs?

"Iris?" Geraline's voice had softened, and a swirl of worry ribboned through it. "What's going on with you?"

"Nothing. Really," she lied, resolutely unwilling to bare her soul now. "Just tired."

"You're excited about Jolie, right? I mean, that's a big one. I hope you realize that."

What could Iris say? If she admitted her reluctance to spend three years in France, Geraline would hound her daily trying to bolster her spirits, which would only have the opposite effect. "It'll be fine, but right now I'm in desperate need of relaxation, and that's all I'm thinking about. I just…I need these six weeks off to recharge." That was as honest as she could be. "Don't worry, I'll go to the opening with that asshat Antoine, so stop sucking up."

Gerri didn't. "I appreciate the team player attitude, Iris. I really do. I know more than anyone how hard you work, and I promise I won't spring anything else on you after this until I see you at De Gaulle Airport in six weeks. Okay?"

Iris smiled wearily. "I'm holding you to that."

"Deal. What are your plans for vacation?"

"I haven't set any yet," she said. Sleeping and visiting her friends and family were high on the list. Anything to take her mind off her troubles and doubts. "I'm sure I'll find something enthralling to keep me busy."

"Good. You get over this hurdle with Antoine, and you're home free." Geraline chuckled. "Try to have a good time tonight. I'll call you tomorrow and see how it went. Oh"—she clucked with regret—"one more teensy little thing. I told Antoine he could stay there at the house tonight—"

"What?" Iris's backbone went rigid. Geraline always

dropped bombs just when Iris had let her guard down. "Damnit, Geraline!"

"Listen, you don't have to entertain him—the house is plenty big enough for the two of you—but please don't kill him before he boards his flight to Milan tomorrow morning. That's all I ask."

"But—"

"Talk to you later, Iris. Play nice." *Click.*

Fuck. Iris slammed her cell phone onto the table next to the chaise. She hated being manipulated, yet it seemed to be happening more frequently lately. Or maybe she'd just grown less tolerant of it.

A honeysuckle-scented breeze from the gardens wafted up and caught her attention. She turned toward it, hoping it would wash over her face and dispel some of her annoyance, but a movement below caught her eye. She stretched up to investigate. Aha, Geraline's new gardener, Torien. She'd just emerged from behind the gazebo, freshly cut cream and red roses cradled in her sun-browned arms.

Iris floundered up out of the chair with all the grace of a woman with her ass stuck in a barrel. Smoothing her dress, she tiptoed to the railing for a better look, even though doing so made her feel like a voyeuristic tramp. But, holy crap, if anything was worth gawking at… Iris bit her lip.

Torien's sleeveless shirt was buttoned low enough to expose a good portion of her sports bra, like she'd thrown it over her body as an afterthought. Sweat glistened on her defined delts and the exposed area of her chest. Mud caked the bottoms of her worn jeans and work boots. Her callused hands—*Lord, get a load of those hands*—were clearly unafraid of hard, honest, sweaty work.

"*Hijole…*" Iris watched Torien walk in lanky strides to the side of the potter's cottage and lay the roses gently on a workbench. Bending, she cranked open the garden hose spigot, removed her shirt, and proceeded to splash cold water over her face and chest. She seemed oblivious to the water drenching her baby blue sports bra until her nipples stood at delectable attention, unmindful of the fact that streams traversed the hard planes of her abs to soak into the waistband of those faded, just-baggy-enough-to-be-hella-sexy jeans.

Iris's throat constricted. *Oh...my freaking God.* She could use a little cold splash herself.

If the designers had any sense at all, they'd hire real women like Torien to model their underwear rather than emaciated, vacant-eyed teenage girls. They'd make a killing.

Torien twisted the faucet closed, then arched and stretched, fists kneading the strong, clearly sore, muscles of her lower back.

Iris pressed a hand to her swirling tummy. Nothing compared to the look of hard, physical work on a woman. She wondered what someone like Torien daydreamed about while she dug her hands in the cool, black soil. Certainly not money and designer suits and *image.*

Iris hadn't met Torien in person yet, though she'd heard the head housekeeper and one of the young cooks tittering about her the other night. Now she understood why. Torien was one hundred percent unassuming hotness. Dark. Gorgeous. And awfully tall. At an inch short of six feet herself, Iris appreciated Torien's stature. Not that she didn't find petite women attractive, mind you. But every once in a while, she yearned for an even playing field.

Iris tilted her head to the side and studied Torien's solid, shapely form, strictly for comparison's sake. Yep. They'd be just about eye to eye, mouth to mouth, chest to—

Torien's hot, direct gaze flicked to Iris's and held, as though drawn by Iris's unabashed thoughts and brazen scrutiny. Yikes. Iris was full-on ogling the woman. She *knew* she was ogling, knew she'd been busted. Still, she couldn't make herself stop.

Instead, she ventured a goofy little finger wave and a

tremulous "caught me lookin'" smile. For a moment, Torien's eyes widened with something akin to surprise, recognition, maybe even shock. But no smile followed. No wave. The muscles in her jaw moved before she hastily threw her shirt back on and jerked her attention back to her work.

Iris released a breath of absolute admiration. Now, *there* was a woman.

The contrast between Torien and Iris's ex-girlfriend, a pop/rock singer on the platinum rise, was staggering. Hard to believe the two of them belonged to the same species, let alone the same gender. Still, as mesmerizing as Geraline's new gardener was, that annoyingly familiar bedfellow—guilt—assailed Iris again. Torien wasn't a piece of meat, and regardless of her world-class, pulsating sexual draw, Iris shouldn't have stared at her like that.

❖

Torien shouldn't have stared at her like that. Damnit.

Regret dug at her conscience.

Hours had passed since Torien had seen none other than Iris Lujan on the *terraza*, but no matter. It wasn't nearly long enough for her to have erased the startling image from her mind. Unbelievable. Iris was a lady, not some *páginas centrales* to be gaped at by *la jardinera*. Was she a fool? She could not afford to lose this job.

Jaw clenched, Torien drove the trowel into the night-cooled soil, hoping the extra work would dispel her slamming self-reproach. She focused on gratitude for how good she had it with this job—a fact about which her *amigas* never failed to remind her. But she had earned this job honestly, and she loved it. She did good work—always. She split her time between the small, shared apartment in town and the gardener's *cabaña* here, both of which disgraced the shack of her childhood. The money she earned was more than her father—God rest his soul—had ever been able to bring home, more than Torien's friends made with their back-breaking, mind-numbing labor. Torien sent a tidy sum to *Mamá* each month while holding a bit aside for herself and her own dreams for the future. But she'd never be able to reach for her dreams if *Señora* Moreno fired her.

¡Maldita sea! She shouldn't have stared at Iris.

Sitting back on her haunches, Torien tilted her face to the iridescent moonlight and recalled the ethereal look of Iris standing there in the sunshine. That famous long black hair Torien had imagined touching, lush curves displayed to perfection in some sort of wispy, swirling white dress.

Torien knew who she was. How could she not? Iris Lujan was equal to Marilyn Monroe in the eyes of the young men—and many of the young women—from her hometown in *México*. Iris's magazine photos and covers had decorated the walls of the small room she shared with her *hermanita*, Madeira—and the walls of many of their peers as well. Torien had tacked hers up to be admired while she fell asleep.

Being this close to the woman from those magazine photographs was surreal. Unimaginable. Iris was such…a woman, perfect in all the ways that made Torien thankful, once again, to be a lesbian. Iris had smiled and waved, and a tremor of pure shock unlike anything she'd ever felt before had spiked through Torien. All she could do was stare, although every fiber of her soul had whispered, "Look away! Show respect!" She'd been sweaty and work-worn, in no shape to interact with anyone, much less a woman of Iris's caliber. She could only hope she had not offended her. Shaking her head, Torien lifted the trowel and again impaled the earth, pulling up a cone of rich soil, which she set aside. She had another flat of bulbs to plant before she could call it a night.

A prickle at the back of her neck jerked her gaze to the torchlit *terraza*.

There she stood—*again*. Iris.

Stomach lurching, Torien scrambled to her feet. Iris Lujan leaned against the railing, wearing some shimmery garment in variegated reds that highlighted her famous curves painfully well. Torien could not believe their paths would cross twice in one day. She glanced up at the stars, meaning to thank the brightest one for the good fortune, then she heard it.

Sniff, sniff.

Wait a minute— Torien frowned. Was she crying?

A sharp protective instinct propelled her closer, but she soon remembered herself and moved behind a rose trellis so as not to be seen. Iris *was* crying. The ridiculous urge to go to her, to console her, overwhelmed Torien. But before she could take a step, a well-dressed *hombre rubio* sauntered up to her side and held something out to her. The beauty glanced at the man—really just a boy, and none too masculine, if she were honest. Torien turned away.

Iris's lover? She'd heard rumors Iris was a lesbian, had seen paparazzi photos of her holding hands with a female musician. Torien had held the notion of Iris Lujan being a lesbian in her mind and heart, but…perhaps it was not true? The blond boy looked the lucky rich type who would date a famous model simply because he felt…entitled.

Just as well.

Torien's family had always told her she dreamed too big, and this idiotic…*distraction* over Iris underscored the point. Despite Torien's unexpected physical proximity to her, their lives were, and always would be, worlds apart.

It was not Torien's place to comfort Iris Lujan.

It would *never* be her place.

❖

"What are you crying about?" Antoine sneered, in that infuriating, affected, half-British, half-LA club-boy accent. "At least you looked good in the picture, which is all that really counts. Drink this." He thrust the crystal lowball glass closer, a practiced—probably in the mirror—smirk twisting his well-photographed Greek statue lips. "Top-of-the-line stuff, compliments of our manager."

Iris swiped at her eyes and skirted past him, wrapping her arms around her torso. Why'd he have to follow her out to the terrace? Couldn't he find something shiny and amuse himself for a few minutes so she could have solitude to lick her wounds?

Swear to God, she could rip Geraline limb from limb for letting Antoine stay here. But who was Iris to say Little Mister Brainless and Pretty couldn't? It wasn't *her* mansion. "I don't want any Scotch. What I really want," she added, in her best take-a-hint tone, "is to be left alone."

She shivered, still nauseated over the fiasco at the restaurant opening. One of the news reporters had thrust a sleazy tabloid in front of her. The article teaser smack in the center of the first page claimed she'd had a boob job and a nose job, which she paid off with sexual favors. Were they for real?

Granted, *she* knew it wasn't true. Anyone who knew and loved her would recognize trash journalism at its bottom-feeding worst. But it still had to hurt her parents to read such garbage. And what if people did believe it? It just reinforced the false image of her as a vain, empty, brainless model. She groaned, unable to hold it back.

"Oh, Christ, drama queen. Blow it off." Antoine drained his glass, then dumped the ice cubes into the glass he'd filled for Iris. His eyes had that glassy, off-focus quality that had caused him problems on more than one assignment. She could only hope he'd pass out. "You know what Geraline says: no publicity is bad publicity." Antoine flashed an insipid grin.

She gaped at him, incredulous. Did he have an original thought in his head? "I'm not talking about publicity. This is my life they're messing with. My integrity."

"Same diff." His disinterested gaze combed her head to foot, then scraped back up, settling squarely in the area of her plunging neckline. "So, tell me, just between friends"—he dipped his chin, eyes fixated—"*are* those puppies really yours?"

Her anger revved, and her French-manicured nails cut into her palms. "First of all, Antoine, you and I are not friends—don't flatter yourself. If we didn't share management, we wouldn't even know each other. Secondly, it's none of your damned business, so kindly fuck off. Lastly—" She caught herself, pressing her lips together to regain her composure. She didn't need to rip him a new one; she merely wanted to explain that, despite the fact she made her living with her appearance, her body wasn't public domain.

Actually—what was she thinking? This was Antoine.

She didn't have to explain squat.

"You know? Let's leave it at kindly fuck off. I'm going to bed."

"Need any company?" He grinned like a kid who'd just found a filthy twenty-dollar bill on the bus station floor and planned to use it for a quickie blow job.

An unladylike snort escaped before she could hold it back. She'd been without a woman for a while now, but she wasn't even close to desperate enough to sleep with a man. Or a *boy*. "Not in this lifetime."

"Well, *par-doe-nay moi*," he said, as if he'd been doing her a favor by offering to sleep with her. He formed the shape of a "W" with his thumbs and forefingers, mouthing the word "whatever" in true Millennial style.

Seething, Iris set her jaw and brushed past him, heading as quickly as she could through the house. She wasn't tired and didn't relish hiding out in her room for the night. But she couldn't tolerate another moment in Antoine's presence, and Geraline had left her without options. If experience was any indication, however, Antoine the Annoying would trail her, like a simple cow heading down the slaughter chute, anywhere but to her bedroom.

As she passed through the massive, arched foyer, she caught a glimpse of the bright moon framed in the leaded glass window that flanked the carved wooden door. Her breath caught. Moonlight bathed the earth in a silvery glow. The night breeze fluttered the sweeping branches of the weeping willow. She released a long, slow breath.

That's what she needed. Fresh air and moonlight and distance from the big blond oaf. A quick walk through the gardens would calm her mind. She reached for the doorknob just as Antoine's voice floated up from some distance behind her.

"Where you going?"

"Nowhere."

His steps quickened on the marble floor. "I thought you were going to bed? Wait! I'll go with you."

"Be right back." Shooting a glance over her shoulder, she scrambled out the door into the safety of darkness. She clung to the bushes, her eyes trained on the front door. It didn't open. After about a minute, Iris crept around the estate grounds, careful to cling to the shadows in case Antoine changed his mind and followed her out. No sense taking chances.

Halfway to the gardens, she removed her sling-back Louboutin stilettos—equal parts gorgeous and impractical—which were slowing her progress, and trashed them behind a shrub. Peering around the corner of the house, she spied the terrace from which she'd just fled. Damn. Antoine had returned there, leaning on the railing. She could hide in the gazebo where he wouldn't be able to see her, but she had to *get* to the gazebo first. With the bright moonlight, the crystal-studded bodice of her cocktail dress would cast reflections like a freaking disco ball. She could only hope Antoine was too plastered by now to notice.

In one mad break, she dashed from the side of the house into the darkest part of the garden and paused, panting. Man, she needed more aerobic exercise. She peeked back to determine whether she'd been seen. Antoine didn't seem to have noticed. Shoving wayward strands of her hair out of her face, she estimated the distance to the gazebo. One hundred feet, maybe less. With one last check of Antoine, she puffed out her cheeks and launched.

Conscious of thorns and branches with the potential to grab at her silk chiffon skirt, she hiked the soft material even higher on her thighs. Not that she cared if it got ruined, since the designer had sent it free of charge, and she'd never be able to wear it again anyway. It would always be associated with tabloid hell night, both in her mind and the collective mind of the paparazzi.

She stealthed her way through the fragrant garden, from flowering tree to expertly shaped bush to blossom-dripping trellis, pausing each time she reached cover to make sure she'd gone undetected. In one final rush, she scurried to the gazebo and sank onto the stairs. Her feet stung from the crushed Caribbean seashell path—one of Geraline's splurges—but Iris didn't care. She was alone. Finally.

Relief came sharply—but so did an unexpected wave of tears. Not the plink-plunk kind, but a shoulder-racking torrent complete with loud sobs she muffled by burying her face in her palms. Where had this come from? The tabloid story bothered her, sure, but these tears seemed to be bubbling up from a deeper place. She shouldn't *be* so unhappy.

To hell with this career.

The momentary surge of anger empowered her to square her shoulders…but self-doubt just as swiftly rounded them again. As if she had the guts to declare a mutiny on the only career she'd ever known. Ha! What would people think if she turned her back on a lifestyle so many women dreamed of having? Not to mention the fact she had no other skills, zippo training at anything.

Scared? Damn right, she was scared.

Her father had always said, *entrada de caballo y salida de burro*—Dad's quirky way of reminding her to finish what she started. And he was right—Iris *ought* to do just that. But just how did a person know for certain when something was finished?

Iris Lujan, the public figure, was known as brash, bold, and brimming with cutting-edge confidence. Her publicity people pushed the image. So did Geraline. But Iris, the small-town Colorado girl? Whole different story. What would people think if they knew how unsure of herself she often felt? How completely unsettled? How she worried, every day, that there was nothing but emptiness hidden behind the magazine page image? That she truly was nothing more than 110 pounds of horseflesh on the bidding block? What would everyone say if they learned the super-powerful supermodel Iris-L wasn't certain she even knew herself anymore?

CHAPTER TWO

Torien froze when Iris tore through the gardens as if demons nipped at her heels. She seemed oblivious to Torien's presence, but Torien had definitely seen *her*. From the shiny, wispy dress that looked like some rare island flower in full bloom, to those endless tanned legs she'd exposed by lifting the flounce of her short skirt even higher, Iris running barefoot through the gardens was a visual Torien would not soon forget. A lovely dark angel in flight...

But now...she wept. The plaintive, hollow sound pierced straight to Torien's soul. Had Iris and her *novio rubio* argued? Why else would she flee to the garden, shoeless and crying? Torien inched closer, wishing she'd taken the time earlier to scrub the mud from her hands and brush her hair. For the second time that day, self-consciousness about her disheveled appearance clutched at Torien. Her heart sank. She straightened her shirt and wiped damp, soil-covered palms along the sides of her jeans. She didn't know quite how to console this broken *ángel*, didn't have the words. But as a self-respecting woman, she simply must try.

Torien's throat tightened to bone dry, and all the English she had learned seemed to vanish from her brain—*poof*. She stayed to the shadows as she approached the gazebo, and stopped when she was close enough to smell the lemon basil she had planted along the edges of the gazebo steps mingling with the spicy tang of Iris's perfume.

But still, the proper words didn't come. Damn.

Mamá would know how to handle a crying woman. So would her sisters—especially Madeira, whose charming, flirtatious ways could have almost any woman eating straight from her palms within minutes. Torien, however, desperately wished Iris were a wilting plant or a tomato bug—hell, even root rot.

Those, she could handle. In her sleep. But a crying woman...?

Torien stood partially behind the trellis of climbing hydrangea and clematis, and warred with herself whether she should remain there, or be an adult and show her face in the open. She did not wish to frighten Iris, nor did she want to intrude.

Afraid of a woman, Toro? whispered her conscience, wryly. Madeira would love to tease her about that.

Torien scowled.

That wasn't it. She didn't fear women.

But this wasn't just any woman. Iris was famous.

Despite that, Torien took a deep breath and spoke softly. *"Perdóname, señora? ¿Qué haces?"*

Iris gasped and leapt to her feet, pressing a palm to her chest. Her wide eyes took in Torien's clearly unexpected presence, then her shoulders drooped and her eyelids fluttered shut. When she opened them again, she said, "Torien. You scared me."

Torien held out a hand to reassure her. "I only come to see if you are well."

"I-I thought I was alone." Iris sank back on to the steps and smeared tears from her cheeks, looking slightly chagrined. To Torien's relief, Iris did not order her away.

She knows my name, Torien realized with a jolt. It both surprised and pleased her. She moistened her lips and moved from behind the trellis to stand beside Iris. The moonlight cast bluish shadows across Iris's face, accentuating the high cheekbones and proud nose that Torien—and most of the world—knew so well. But, somehow, in person, Iris looked more vulnerable. Less intimidating. *Real.* "Why do you cry?"

Iris peered up, seeming to measure the question. "I d-don't know," she whispered, her words trembly and fast. "I mean, I know, but it's a long story. Antoine's an idiot, and then that stupid tabloid story. My life just…sucks. It's hard to explain and would probably bore you half to death anyway or make you think I'm an ungrateful brat, so"—she waved a listless hand—"just don't worry about it. I'm sorry to have interrupted you."

"Please, can you…" The heat of embarrassment seared Torien's body. She clenched her fists in frustration.

Iris's watery, questioning eyes lifted to Torien's face.

Torien hated to ask, but if she meant to console Iris, she had no choice. "Can you speak more slowly?" Torien's mouth twisted to the side and she shrugged. "My English is still…like a child's, yet I wish to hear your words through the ears of a woman."

To Torien's surprise, a small smile lit Iris's troubled face. "I'm so sorry. How rude of me. I can use Spanish if you—"

"No, please. I like the practice. Just…not so fast. You Americans—" Torien made a yapping motion with her hand and smiled ruefully.

Iris's eyes warmed, Torien noticed, really seeming to see her. For a split second, every detail that separated Torien's life from Iris's seemed to disappear. That she wore thrift store worker's jeans caked with dried mud while Iris wore a dress so lovely, it must have cost thousands of dollars, didn't matter. Torien wasn't simply a poor gardener from *México* struggling to make her way in a new country. Iris wasn't simply a famous model straight from the slick magazine pages. They were simply…two women sharing a conversation in the moonlit garden.

If I could freeze the moment, Torien thought.

Iris patted the step next to her. "Sit with me, Torien."

Torien hesitated, and their differences rushed back into stark focus like she should've known they would. She glanced toward the *terraza* for Iris's boyfriend. "I should not."

Iris's eyes implored Torien, luminous in the moonlight. "Please? I don't bite. I just…really need to talk to a normal person right now."

How could anyone deny her? Pushing away the nagging fear she might be overstepping her boundaries, Torien sat, careful to maintain a respectable distance between them. For the second time in the short moments since Torien had first seen Iris, her dark garden angel, words failed to formulate into anything coherent in her mind.

Think, Toro.

She had never been a woman of many words, but this was absurd. She stared at the prospering bed of love-in-a-mist across the path from where they sat and racked her brain for what she should say next.

Thankfully, the beauty saved her the trouble. She stuck out her hand. "We haven't properly met. I'm Iris Lujan."

Torien stared at Iris's soft palm, dismayed by the thought of dirtying it, yet thrilled by the prospect of touching her all the same. She finally slid her hand against Iris's. "I…I know who you are. I am Torien Pacias."

"I know who you are, too."

To Torien's relief, Iris didn't seem to mind her callused, soil-covered palm. Instead, she smiled, though her eyes remained troubled. "What are you doing out here so late?"

Torien gestured to the freshly turned soil. "Planting bulbs. They prefer the cool of night to the burning sun." Truthfully, Torien had been spending so much time with her volunteer gardening project in *el barrio*, she had not arrived at Moreno's until late afternoon, just before she had seen Iris that first time on the *terraza*. But that was a detail she didn't wish to share. Torien could feel Iris's thoughtful gaze on the side of her face.

"I saw the roses you cut this afternoon."

Iris paused, and Torien wanted to deny she had seen Iris, too. Stared at her. Ignored her friendly wave.

"They were beautiful," Iris added.

"*Gracias*. Hybrid tea roses." She paused, swallowing thickly. "I still had…much work to do, when I saw you there." Torien motioned to the *terraza*. It was all she could manage as an apology.

"That's okay," Iris said. "I shouldn't have spied on you."

She pointed toward the big house, hoping to turn the conversation back to Iris's unexpected presence in the garden. "Did you and your boyfriend fight, *señora*?"

"Boyfriend? Antoine?" Iris reeled back, looking horrified. "Please. The twit is *not* my boyfriend."

"Forgive me. I assumed…"

"I don't…date men, Torien. Only women. When I do date, that is."

This pleased Torien more than it should have. "But you are troubled." It was more of an observation than a question. *"¿Por qué?"*

Iris sighed. "It's a long story."

"I have nothing but time." She shrugged, even though truthfully her time seemed in short supply lately. "Ask the bulbs."

Iris chuckled, but ended with a groan. Then she just sat, absentmindedly twirling a simple silver ring she wore on the middle finger of her right hand. Round and round and round. Staring off into the distance, her words low and monotone, she asked, "Do you ever wonder if you're on the right track in life?"

Not quite sure what answer the vague question demanded, Torien waited. If Iris was anything like Torien's little sisters, she would fill any silences with words. The gamble paid off.

Iris quickly added, "I mean, you're a gardener, and you seem like you love what you do."

"Sí." Torien cast Iris a sidelong glance. "It's a good job."

"Don't you ever experience moments of self-doubt?"

Iris ignored the long strands of her hair that the soft

breeze carried over her cheek, but Torien was struck with the overwhelming urge to brush it back. She refrained, but the effort distracted her.

"Have you ever worried that you aren't living the life you were meant to live?" Iris added.

Torien had not expected deep questions such as these. She knew she would rather be home in *México*, if that was what Iris meant. But she also knew it was impossible. "Everyone has those types of doubts, *señora*. It is part of being *humano*, no?"

Iris sat in silence for a moment, seeming to consider the words. "Even you, Torien? You don't seem doubtful. What would you be if you didn't garden?"

"I would be without money," she teased, hoping to ease some of the anguish on Iris's face.

To Torien's pleasure, Iris's features softened. "You know what I mean. What do you dream about?"

This time, Torien knew exactly what Iris asked. Sure, she wished she could bring her *mamá* and baby sisters here to live as a family, or better yet, go to them. She wished the *Americanos* she had encountered in this country would not avert their eyes when she passed, as if her mere existence in their world was unwelcome. But not all of them acted this way, and so many other people had far greater problems than hers. People she knew, cared for.

Torien raised her unwavering gaze. "I live in a comfortable house and have clothes on my back, food on my table. I am able to see to the needs of *mi familia*. A humble woman should be satisfied with such blessings, no?"

Iris blinked, looking startled. "Is your family here?"

"Some of them."

"Oh." She traced the contours of Torien's face with her lovely green eyes, her throat moving on a slow swallow. "How many children do you have?"

Surprise pulled a short laugh from inside Torien. If Iris thought she had time to date, let alone find a woman and raise a family, she had no concept of Torien's life. "No, you misunderstand. I am speaking of *mi mamá y mis hermanas*. I am not married."

"Oh. I'm sorry. I just assumed…" Iris didn't finish the thought.

"Like you, I also only date women," Torien added in a shy tone. She didn't know why she felt the need to tell Iris, but… there it was. The heat of embarrassment rose up her neck.

Iris smiled. "So, who is here with you? Your sisters?"

Torien nodded. "Just one. Madeira. She is twenty-four, but acts more like eighteen."

Iris laughed softly.

"My younger sisters live back home with my *mamá*."

"How many sisters?"

Torien angled a playful look of reproach in Iris's direction. "We are supposed to be talking about you."

"I'm just curious. If you don't want to talk about your family—"

"No, I—" Torien released a breath. If Iris wanted to hear about her *familia*, she would happily tell her. The thought of her two mischief-making *hermanitas*, mirror images of one another, brought a smile. "Two more. Raquel and Reina. They are *mellizas*, no? Twins?"

Iris nodded. "Identical?"

"Yes. Special little girls, but *malcriado*—how do you say?"

"Spoiled rotten?"

"Exactly."

Iris waved away the words. "Oh, now, everybody says that about their little sisters. I bet I'd adore them. All of them."

"You would," Torien admitted. Everyone adored the twins, and women especially were easily sucked in by Madeira's flirtatious charm. Homesickness jabbed Torien. She tried to deflect the blade, but here in the moonlight, a stab of pure longing pierced her soul.

The hardest thing she had ever done was leave her mother and sisters and set off with Madeira for *los Estados Unidos*. But they had been unable to earn enough money in their small town and had left to honor their father, who would have done the same thing had he lived long enough for the opportunity to present itself. They were not uneducated people, the Pacias sisters. There just were no jobs. As the eldest daughter, Torien took it as her duty to maintain the family, and she knew she'd have a better chance of it here.

She had dragged her charming, fun-seeking hermanita along, knowing they could do more for the family together than apart. Besides—her lips twitched with tired amusement—Madeira needed a keeper even more than the twins, and Torien hadn't wanted to saddle *Mamá* with the extra responsibility. Little mosquito. She'd dated her way through their hometown, leaving a backlog of women fighting over her and Torien trying her best to sweep up the debris. Madeira had been only too happy to escape.

Torien shook her head.

"What are you thinking about?" Iris asked.

"Home," she replied simply.

"And that makes you sad?"

Torien paused. "It's hard to be away from loved ones."

"Now, that," Iris said, "I completely understand."

Shake it off, Toro. Madeira was forever telling Torien to "lighten up," while Torien always got after Madeira about "getting serious."

They complemented each other.

In her heart, Torien knew she belonged in *México*, where she was just another person, rather than a "foreigner." She missed that feeling of being…simply another thread in the quilt of humanity. Though she liked it here, liked the life she was building, Torien wasn't sure she would ever feel as invisibly comfortable in the United States as she had back home. Even those called "Mexican Americans" were often people Torien did not recognize, people who might *physically* resemble her, but nothing more. There were cultural similarities, *sí*. But where it truly counted, the Mexican Americans were American.

She was *Mexicana*.

She did not begrudge the differences, but wouldn't deny their existence either. Torien slid a quick glance at Iris, an excellent example of the difference. Iris was a *Mexican American*, for sure, but clearly belonging to a world outside Torien's experience. One might as well compare a carrot with a rose. They both grew in the earth, but beyond that...well, even her charming little sister wouldn't get very far by bringing a beautiful woman a bouquet of...carrots.

The image lightened her thoughts, and Torien shoved aside the melancholy. Iris hadn't asked her to share the gazebo step in glum silence with her face long like a mule's. She picked up the string of their conversation easily. "I miss them. Raquel and Reina are easy to love. Beautiful girls, but teenagers now, no? That time is always difficult."

Iris nodded, then stared up at the moon. She smoothed her palms up and down her arms as though chilled. "I don't have siblings. Though my two best friends are like sisters." Her voice sounded distant, as if her thoughts were miles away. "Still, it's probably not the same as a real sister. Or a twin."

"There is nothing so close as a twin," Torien said. *Except a lover, if you find the right one.* Her stomach flipped, and she forced herself to follow Iris's gaze, noting a thin wisp of clouds waltzing with *la luna*. The insanity of this moment struck her. Was she really sitting beneath the stars talking with none other than world-famous Iris Lujan? It hardly seemed possible. Torien inhaled the familiar earthy smells of the garden to prove she was not dreaming, and with them came the spice of Iris's perfume, the incomparable feminine sweetness of her skin. This moment *was* real. And one of the best, most surreal, in Torien's life.

Iris pulled her long, slim legs up close to her body and wrapped her arms around them. She rested her cheek on her knees

and studied Torien for long moments. Just when Torien began to
squirm beneath her stare, Iris lifted her head and reached over to
squeeze Torien's arm. "You're a different sort of woman than I'm
used to."

Torien's stomach contracted with desire from the simple
touch of Iris's warm hand. "We only just met. How can you
know?"

"Trust me, I know." Iris's eyes darkened, looking once again
sad. "You're sitting here talking to me, aren't you? About family.
Normal things. Everything and nothing, all at the same time."

An appropriate response eluded Torien, so she said nothing.
With a decisive breath, Iris stood.

Regret seized Torien. She wasn't ready for Iris to leave.
Time had stilled while they conversed, and Torien's mind had
calmed. She didn't want to let go of the feeling, but angels kept
their own schedules, she supposed. She stood, too, and faced Iris.
For some inexplicable reason, it pleased her that Iris's eyes were
on an equal level with her own.

"Thank you for…listening to me." Iris tucked her lush hair
behind her ears and looked rather chagrined. "Sometimes I get so
caught up in things I feel…ungrounded. I really needed someone
to pull me back to earth."

Torien lifted her arms and let them fall to her sides, feeling
helpless. "But I did nothing, *señora*, except talk about *mi
familia*."

"Well, it has been the best part of my night. Thank you." Iris
tilted her head to one side. "Can you do me one small favor?"

Eat broken glass? Rope the moon? Sell my soul? Standing
there in the fertile garden, drunk on moonlight and Iris's
presence, Torien knew she'd do whatever Iris asked. "Of course.
Anything."

"Call me Iris. When you call me *señora*, it makes me feel
so…separated, if you know what I mean." Her eyes shadowed.
"I've had enough separation in my life already."

Torien understood only too well. "With pleasure…Iris."

Iris smiled. "I like the way you say it. Well, I guess I'll see you around."

"Buenas noches."

Iris looked as if she were waiting for Torien to say more, but no words came. Finally, she added, "I'll be staying here for six weeks. I'm on vacation."

Torien nodded, paused…unsure what the proper response would be. "Enjoy it," she said, wishing her words had more meaning, more depth.

"I'm glad I finally met you, Torien." Iris hesitated, but before Torien knew what had happened, Iris leaned forward and touched her soft lips to Torien's cheek. A brief kiss of gratitude, she supposed, before Iris turned and hurried away in that ethereal red dress and bare feet.

Torien stood there for long moments, the skin on her cheek tingling, dread twirling with awareness in her middle. Iris's words rang in her mind:

See you around.

I'm glad I finally met you.

I'll be here for six weeks.

Señora Moreno had warned Torien there would be many famous people in and out of her home. The boss had left no doubt in Torien's mind that the hired help were expected to keep to their own business. Torien agreed it was the wise choice all the way around, and never gave it much thought. Frankly, there were no famous people she desired to spend time with…until now. Watching Iris's retreating form, so luscious and vulnerable in the moonlight, Torien wished their differences were not so stark, their situation not so unfavorable. Six whole weeks in her intoxicating presence? Would Torien have the strength of will and presence of mind to resist her?

Did she really want to?

Think of your obligations, Toro.

Pressing her lips together, Torien resigned herself to the fact that spending time with Iris wouldn't pay the bills, whereas working for Moreno would. She knew the toll her responsibilities would take on the family if she lost this job over a ridiculous infatuation with an untouchable woman. Torien laughed derisively to herself. Untouchable was an understatement. Like catching sunlight with a butterfly net.

Just as well.

She was only dreaming big again.

Firm in her decision, Torien returned to her knees by the turned garden soil. If Iris sought her out again, Torien had no choice but to avoid her.

Torien could not decide if it was dismay or relief that washed over her when she arrived at the estate several days later and found Iris sitting cross-legged on the bench in front of the small reflective pond. She had thought of her constantly since their unlikely midnight meeting, and seeing her now, caressed by the long, gold fingers of afternoon light, stole Torien's breath. The magazine images truly didn't do the living, breathing woman justice. It wasn't just Iris's obvious photogenic qualities, it was the life that pulsed from her, the honesty. The almost pensive vulnerability—something Torien never expected to see.

Iris glanced up from the book she had been reading and smiled. "You do keep strange hours. Hi."

Remember yourself. She didn't want to repeat patterns she'd learned. Patterns that disgusted her. Responsibility—that was her saving grace. Feeling out of step, Torien took her time maneuvering the paper bag of supplies she picked up at the nursery to her other hip. The crackling of the thick brown paper mirrored the rattle of her nerves. She had replayed their conversation repeatedly, revising her own words, her reactions to Iris. Recreating herself into the confident, sophisticated woman she wished she could be. Now here she sat, and Torien could think of nothing to say.

Typical.

Torien smoothed her free hand through her hair slowly, grappling for her bearings. "Hello, again. I am surprised to see you here."

A tiny line bisected Iris's smooth, regal forehead. "I'm staying here, remember?"

"I meant, here in the garden."

"Ah." Iris looked around, serenity on her face. "I like it. It's peaceful. I definitely need some peace on this vacation."

Nodding, Torien stared at Iris for a moment longer. Then, not knowing what else to do, and hoping to give her this peace she craved, Torien turned and carried the purchases into the cool, dim potter's cottage. She placed fertilizer and a few new tools into the cabinets, then yanked her T-shirt over her head, meaning to change into one of the sleeveless button-up shirts she favored while working. The simple roughness of the cotton T-shirt brushing her flesh felt sensual, and she cursed in a rough whisper. It wasn't the shirt razing Torien's senses, it was Iris. The admission settled like river rock in her gut. She'd be a damned fool if she let Iris get any further under her skin.

With a sigh, she braced her palms wide on the slatted wood counter top and hung her head. Why had Iris come into Torien's space again? To complicate her life? Iris's presence put her *entre la espada y la pared*—between the sword and the wall. Torien could not afford to anger Moreno, a formidable woman, by bothering guests of the estate. Yet she could not bear to send Iris away.

Even spending casual time with Iris skirted the line of propriety, but with Torien's blood running so damn hot every time Iris was near, it nearly crossed the line completely. And could only lead to problems—this, she knew. She had frequent and varied opportunities for uncomplicated female companionship, which was more than she could handle right now. The last thing she needed was a woman like Iris to muddle her brain and rattle her convictions.

Yet Iris had come to *her*.

Torien's heart skipped.

There she sat in the lush, fragrant garden, looking more beautiful than the rarest blossom ever could. Curvy, soft, warm, and painfully feminine. Close enough to touch, though doing so would be about as wise as Torien running her hand over an open flame. Either way, she'd end up getting burned.

Torien's logical, analytical side told her one thing: Iris Lujan spelled danger.

And Torien's explosive reaction to her was the most dangerous part of all.

She wasn't used to playing with fire...

"Torien?"

She spun to find Iris shadowing the doorway of the cottage, one bare foot resting atop the other, hand braced on the doorjamb. Iris's gaze traced down her body, taking in the sports bra and bare stomach, making her feel utterly exposed. She had not realized before how small the potting cottage was, how intimate. It smelled of earth and green. Life. Torien's pulse thrummed in her ears. Reaching for the clean white sleeveless shirt she'd left folded on the cane-back chair in the corner, she punched her arms through the sleeve holes, covering her bare skin as quickly as she could.

"I didn't mean to startle you." Iris's caramel complexion stained with the dusky rose of embarrassment. "And, I'm sorry, I-I didn't know you were..." Iris gestured toward Torien's body, then raked her full bottom lip through her teeth, looking wary, as though Torien meant her harm. Maybe Iris sensed what Torien had been feeling.

She shook her head. "It's okay," Torien said, a little too gruffly. "What do you need?"

Iris's hair spilled over one shoulder, the silky strands brushing against the curve of one breast, all too prominently displayed in the red tank top she wore tucked into low-slung, fitted denim shorts. Speaking of skin, Iris's outfit exposed far too much of hers for Torien's mental well-being. She tried not to focus on it.

Iris crossed her arms beneath her bosoms. "Will it be a problem if I sit in the gardens while you work?"

Torien gazed out the dust-hazed window, trying to seek distance from Iris, from her own traitorous feelings. She had never been more aware of her own visceral reactions, never more distracted by a woman she could never have.

She meant to tell Iris she must go, but found she could not. Torien didn't want Iris to leave. Instead she waved her hand indifferently, and picked up the hedge trimmers. *"Cada perico a su estaca, cada changa a su mecate."*

"I'm…not sure I understand what that means, Tori."

Her stomach contracted as all the breath seemed to push from her lungs. No one called her Tori. Toro, yes, because of her bullheaded nature. But never Tori. Still, she loved the sound of it on Iris's tongue. "A Mexican saying, one of my father's."

Iris laughed softly. "My dad has his favorite sayings, too."

"I think all fathers do. This one, it means…" Torien paused to figure out the simplest translation. "Do what you wish."

Iris blinked. Confusion showed on her face. "O-okay. Thank you."

That settled, Torien expected Iris to leave.

She did not.

Leaning one temple against the doorjamb, she asked, "Have I done something to bother you?"

"Of course not." Torien forced her mouth to smile around the small lie and softened her tone. Torien was bothered, all right. Her nerves danced, sensitized and ready, just beneath her skin. "I just have much work to do." She reminded herself who she was, who Iris was, and where they were, then added politely, "However, you may stay. Of course. The gardens are for the enjoyment of *Señora* Moreno and her guests."

Those green eyes, like spring leaves under ice, assessed Torien unblinkingly. "Geraline is my business manager, you know."

"I did not know." Torien's breaths came only with conscious effort. She shifted position, her boots making a thick sawdust-on-wood sound against the floor. What did Iris expect her to say? "That is...ah...good."

"Yes. I guess so." Iris licked her lips, her gaze flitting through the small cottage to light on anything but Torien. "She takes care of my contracts, assignments. Things like that."

"I see."

Why are you telling me this, Irisíta? You like playing with fire, too?

Heat surged through Torien's veins as she studied Iris. She hoped it didn't show in her eyes.

One sharp inhale through her nose, and Iris said, "Well, anyway..." She pointed toward the bench. With a hesitant turn, she headed down the pale pink, crushed shell path to reclaim her seat.

Unable to stop herself, Torien leaned her spine against the doorjamb, half in the cottage and half out, and watched as each crunching footstep punctuated the sultry sway of Iris's hips. Her mind's eye set the image in slow motion, and she couldn't tear her gaze away.

Damn her human weakness. She did not want to look away, even as she knew she should.

Iris settled on the shaded bench, tucking those long, lean legs beneath her and wiggling into a comfortable position. She looked up, finding Torien studying her from the doorway. That familiar line of concern crinkled her smooth forehead. "Is everything okay?"

Torien decided to answer honestly. "I...don't know."

Iris nodded as though she understood the cryptic words, but Torien knew from her reply she did not. "I won't get in your way. Promise. I'll just sit here and be quiet. And watch, if that doesn't make you too uncomfortable."

Torien couldn't get more uncomfortable than she already was. "*No pierdas cuidado*. You understand?"

"Yes. In slang, we'd say something like…'don't sweat it.' Thank you. I appreciate you letting me watch while you work." Iris's features gentled with sincere relief, and happiness lit her wide, light eyes.

For one suspended, painful moment Torien felt she would do anything in the world to put that look on Iris's face again.

And again.

Iris could be anywhere, with any woman she wanted—or any man, for that matter. Or alone. Yet she'd chosen to be here in the garden with Torien.

It means nothing, Toro.

Even if it had, nothing could come of it.

Iris shooed Torien playfully with her soft, slender hands. "Go on, then. Just act like I'm not here."

The absurdity of her statement smoothed the rough edges off Torien's worry and emboldened her. One corner of her mouth lifted with tired amusement. Torien's pure female core compelled her to say what was on her mind. "I am strong-willed, Irisíta, but pretending not to notice you would be an impossible task for any woman."

Iris's gaze dropped, and she swallowed slowly.

Benevolent vindication soothed Torien as she crossed to the topiary bushes and began to trim. Torien knew she had flustered Iris. But after the physical and emotional havoc Iris had wreaked on her, Torien felt nothing less than justified.

❖

Lord have mercy on her lust-ridden soul, Torien positively reeked, dripped, exuded, *epitomized* raw female sensuality. It wasn't so much the few words she said as the way she said them. The timbre of her voice resonated against Iris's chest like a rough caress, exactly how she instinctively knew Torien's hands would feel on her skin.

Relief that their conversation had ended shook through Iris.

Seeing Torien standing there in the doorway of the shed, half of her face sunlit, the other half in shadows, Iris didn't think she could eke out one more intelligent word if her life depended on it. As if confronting that toned, sun-browned, half-naked torso inside the potting cottage hadn't been taxing enough. Iris had reeled as though someone had planted a perfect uppercut on her jaw, but she played it off. Torien, so endearing, had lunged for that sleeveless white shirt like Iris's gaze had been an unwelcome touch, and still Iris hadn't had the human decency to turn away.

She couldn't.

The pristine shirt, ragged where the sleeves had been torn off, had smelled like bleach and sunlight and hardworking woman, and deep inside Iris, something primal swirled. She wasn't ashamed to admit Torien made her...want. That last look Torien had given her from the doorway, as if she were holding back—just barely—from running those rough hands all over Iris's body, didn't help matters much.

Iris's blood had hammered in her ears and she couldn't seem to pull air into the deepest part of her lungs. She just hoped Torien hadn't noticed her utter lack of cool.

Several minutes later, when she'd regained her composure, she pretended to read while surreptitiously watching Torien shape the topiary bushes. Torien wielded the trimmer meticulously, like an artist, and the muscles in her arms flexed with each careful twist and turn. Those weren't gym muscles, they were real. Work-hewn and completely beguiling. Torien blended so naturally with the growing things around them.

So fresh. So female. *So real.*

Tori was the type of woman you could imagine making love just by looking at her. Slow-motion imagining, of course.

Iris sighed.

Okay, so it wasn't just the peacefulness of the gardens that had drawn Iris back. She was curious about this sexy, enigmatic *Mexicana.* Torien seemed...so alive. So *normal.* Iris didn't know Torien, true enough. But she wondered if she should try to change that. The circles in which she'd moved over the past decade didn't facilitate contact with truly "average" women—average in the best sense of the word. Those she did meet were usually too intimidated by that big, immobilizing illusion—fame—to do more than gawk or smile nervously from a distance. Whenever Iris did meet an interested woman, she found herself assessing for ulterior motives. Was the woman drawn to the real her, or the hype? If her dating track record proved anything, the hype seemed a lot more alluring than the quite average woman behind it.

Torien, on the other hand, didn't seem the least bit fazed by the "Iris Lujan" hype, nor did she seem to have many preconceived notions about her. Unfortunately, Torien didn't seem altogether thrilled by her attention, either.

A smile of irony curved Iris's lips, and she buried her face in her book to hide it. Murphy's damn Law, in action.

If Geraline were to ask about her vacation plans now, she would have a whole different answer. She wanted to get to know Gerri's enigma of a gardener, and she had six weeks to do so. Watching Torien work wasn't nearly enough. Iris wanted more. But she was nothing if not patient. She would bide her time, connect with Tori on *her* terms…just as soon as she figured out what those were. Iris bit back another smile and pretended to be engrossed in her book. She hadn't felt this kind of fire in the belly for years.

CHAPTER THREE

She had returned to the gardens every day, her presence simultaneously pleasing Torien and testing her strength of will. Saturday—exactly eight days after Iris had turned her life upside down—dawned warm, then quickly shot up to inferno status. Heat-hazed morning sun rays seared Torien's shoulders and head. She had taken a day off from her volunteer work, intent on finishing a new, intricate flower bed at Moreno's. She hadn't expected to run into Iris at this time of day, since she usually worked at the estate in the afternoons and evenings, a fact Iris seemed to have keyed in on almost immediately. But ten minutes after she'd parked the pickup in the back drive, Iris had ambled out to the garden. They'd greeted each other briefly, cheerfully; nothing more.

Two hours into Torien's work, sweat beaded her brow and rolled down her neck, setting her on edge. She desperately wished to remove her shirt and work in her sports bra alone, but every time she almost yanked the shirt over her head, she remembered Iris and the incident in the potting shed. Torien would quickly find herself picturing *Iris's* urgent fingers removing the shirt, Iris pressing those soft, full lips to her heated chest and shoulders. Her body would respond to this little fantasy despite direct orders from her brain to the contrary.

Damnit.

Ever since she'd met Iris, her blood throbbed with need and her mind wandered into places far too wanton for her own good. Or Iris's.

Torien's awareness of Iris from the moment she'd claimed her spot on the bench earlier was especially acute. That familiar way her hair obscured her face when she bent forward over her book. The sunshine glinting off her glossed lips, which she absently tapped with her index finger as she read. The unbelievable creaminess of her skin and its powdery scent, which somehow managed to carry on the breeze and overpower the riot of garden scents, as if just to distract, disrupt, and draw Torien.

How much was one woman expected to take?

The only consolation was the fact that Iris seemed as restless as Torien felt. In between long stints of reading, Iris prowled the garden, barefooted and wearing one of those long, floaty sundresses she favored, this one as blue as the Colorado sky. A deep V in the back exposed perfect caramel skin to the sun's kiss and confirmed Torien's suspicion that she wore no bra. *¡Ay!* Sexy without even trying. How did she do that?

Seemingly lost in thought, Iris studied plants, squatted ever so gracefully to peer into the shiny gazing ball perched atop a brass sculpture at the center of the rock garden, drew small designs in the soil with her toes—an activity that struck Torien as breathtakingly sensual. She watched in her peripheral vision as Iris puttered around the *cabaña*, stooping to sniff a blossom or caress a soft petal between her fingers.

Enough, Torien thought, so preoccupied by Iris's luminous presence that she could hardly work. This was clearly miserable for both of them, and perhaps she merely needed to release Iris from whatever obligation she felt to be there. She must let Iris know she was welcome to return to the air-conditioned rooms of the mansion. God knew Torien would if she could. She stood, stretching the fatigue out of her lower back, wishing it were as simple to purge Iris from her brain. "Are you bored, Iris, or just miserably hot like I am?"

Iris spun toward her, smiled, wrapped her hands in a knot behind her. "A little of both, I think. Am I bothering you?"

God, yes. Yes, yes, yes. She strove for diplomacy with her answer. "I simply don't wish for you to be bored." Torien smoothed sweat from one temple, then the other with the back of her hand, her eyes never leaving Iris's face. "Have you nowhere else to be?"

"Nowhere else I'd *rather* be."

Confusion about the contradiction of this answer, in light of the previous one, must have showed on Torien's face.

Lifting her palms, Iris rushed to explain. "What I mean is, I'm not bored with the garden or with...you." Her lashes lowered. "It's more with...life in general. Hard to explain."

Torien wondered if this general life restlessness had had any bearing on Iris's tears the first night they'd met. "If you would like to talk about it, I would welcome the diversion from the heat."

"Oh...I don't know. I hate to bother you with my problems. They're not important anyway." She tucked the long sweep of her hair behind her ear, then picked her way around a bed of purple coneflower, stopping at the edge of the plot in which Torien had been working. "What are you planting here?"

Torien took the change of subject to mean Iris did not wish to unburden herself. *So be it.* Quite honestly, Torien didn't much care what they talked about. *Everything and nothing*...wasn't that how Iris had described the ease of their conversations? "Planting here?" Kneeling by the freshly turned soil, Torien palmed one of the bulbs from a nearby box, bouncing it lightly as she eyed the sky blue nail polish on Iris's lovely toes, the silver rings on the pinkie toes of both feet. "You won't believe me if I tell you."

"Give it a try."

She shook her head ruefully and squinted up. The sun hid directly behind Iris's body, gilding the outline of her black hair in a shimmering glow. With a sting of awareness, Torien noticed how the sunlight also silhouetted Iris's lithe shape through the thin fabric of her dress. Those infamous long legs ended at light-colored bikini underwear shimmering but barely visible, as if beneath water.

What in the hell are you doing, Toro?

She jerked her gaze away, hating herself for having practically undressed Iris with her eyes. Natural for a woman to notice and appreciate, yes. But disrespectful, too. Torien didn't care to treat any woman that way—not her style—but she felt an extra level of respect and protectiveness for Iris.

Focus. She blinked at the rather ugly bulb cradled in her hand, wrapping her fingers tightly around its familiar shape and size. "Ah…I'm planting…irises."

Iris's throaty laughter lapped over Torien like a warm wave, and when their gazes met, Iris's danced with amusement. "I want to be flattered, but first"—she narrowed her eyes playfully—"is it a coincidence?"

"Not really," Torien said. "I admit, I thought of you when I saw them on sale at the nursery. It is late in the season for them, but the price was a bargain. I will give sunshine and water, everything they need for a chance to bloom next spring."

Iris sat down, her dress billowing out on the ground around her like a blue pond. "Poor little bulbs. I wonder why they didn't sell earlier?" She picked up the rough, brownish-gray orb, seeming to weigh it like Torien had, then regarded her across the dark *tierra jardín*. "You think they'll die?"

Torien toyed with the question. "Bulbs are like dreams. You never know if they will flourish until you plant them in the proper soil."

"Mmm." Her eyes glittered. "Poetic. I'm going to remember that."

Torien's cheeks warmed at her teasing tone. "I'll coddle them. See how it goes. It was worth giving them a chance, no?"

Iris studied her for a long moment, expelled a breath. "I don't suppose you would let me help plant these, seeing as how they're my namesake and all that?" She tossed a bulb from hand to hand.

"It would probably cure my boredom, and then we'll both be able to get out of this miserable heat sooner."

Torien pictured those slender, soft hands deep in the soil, long hair slipping over the bare skin of Iris's back like a black satin sheet. If Moreno were here, the answer would have been a resolute no. But *la patrona* was in Italy. Only Torien and this *ángel* were here in the garden, and the scent of Iris's skin did crazy things to Torien's rationality.

She should not encourage Iris's involvement. She knew she should not. They would be working, sweating, breathing, moving, flexing, stretching side by side with their hands buried in the moist, cool soil. Gardening was the closest thing to sex Torien had ever experienced, and bringing Iris into that bubble would be a mistake. She opened her mouth to explain all these reasons and more for Iris to go back to her book, but instead heard herself say, "You are welcome to help if you wish."

"Really?" Excitement illuminated Iris's eyes like sunlight through tender spring leaves.

Torien glanced at the unblemished skin and perfect, short fingernails of Iris's hands, instantly regretting her decision. *Selfish, Toro. This isn't the work for her.*

"If…if you're sure." She jerked her head toward the small potter's shed. "I have gloves in the *sotechado* so you don't damage your hands."

"But you don't wear gloves."

Torien cocked her head to one side and bestowed a droll look. "I am a gardener, Irisíta. You are not."

Seeming slightly surprised by the glove suggestion—and the reminder that she didn't truly belong in the gardens—Iris spread out her hands and stared at them. First the palms, then the backs, her expression pragmatic. "Actually, I would rather feel the earth between my fingers and to hell with the manicure, if it's all the same to you. I'm on vacation. And there's always airbrushing." With a spark of mischief in her expression, she furrowed both hands into the soil up to her wrists, then raised her eyebrows playfully. "If you want to know a secret, I'm a *machetona* at heart."

"No."

"Really. I'm a tomboy from *way* back."

Right. Iris Lujan, a...*machetona.* Torien didn't want to believe it, but part of her did. And loved the idea. "I will...ah... get the gloves in case you change your mind." Torien got to her feet with surprising calmness and retreated to the *sotechado.* She didn't need the gloves, and clearly Iris didn't want them. What Torien really needed was a break from Iris's heady presence, from her scent and softness, her unexpected layers. From the visual images that kept flashing in Torien's head. She knew she was tempting fate every moment she spent in Iris's company, and yet she could not seem to deny herself the pleasure.

You work hard. You deserve the pleasure.

No one will know.

The rationalizations both soothed Torien and drew her like set traps.

She longed to splash cold water on her body, but she didn't dare. Though she didn't imagine Iris would follow her to the potter's cottage again, she would keep all her clothes on while at Moreno's from here on out, just to be safe. She grabbed the gloves from a wall hook and caressed the fingers as if they were Iris's. A controlled sigh eased through her lips. Giving in to her ever-blossoming weakness for Iris's charms would be Torien's undoing. Which could not happen. Her family—no one else—would bear the burden.

That hammer blow of that realization nailed her to the wood slat floor on which she stood. Damnit, infatuation aside, this was not a game. She needed to set the limits of their relationship and make them very clear to Iris without hurting her feelings or snapping the tenuous strings of their new friendship. That was her challenge...and her responsibility.

But it was fine.

If Torien was used to one thing, it was responsibility.

Though Torien hadn't exactly given her a blanket invitation, Iris decided she'd rather ask for forgiveness than permission. So she returned to the garden every day the following week, as if that engraved invitation sat atop her nightstand—or as if she'd been hired—and dug into whatever chore Torien happened to be tackling. If Torien wanted her to leave, she would say so. So far, much to Iris's relief, that hadn't happened.

The biggest shock of this whole get-closer-to-Torien scheme, one she hadn't anticipated whatsoever, was how quickly she grew to love working in the garden—and surprisingly, not entirely because of the time spent with Tori. Thanks to her multi-continental, less-than-grounded lifestyle, she'd never owned or tended a single potted fern, much less a garden that would need constant tender loving care. But as she toiled in the earth alongside Torien, time stilled for her. The first moment a determined but tender green shoot broke through the soil from one of the seeds she'd planted, tears sprung to her eyes. She'd planted, watered, believed.

And it grew.

Amazing.

Sitting on the ground with the sun warming her back, Iris found herself transported back to any number of sunlit days from her childhood; days spent kneeling in the soil with her mom, enjoying the summer heat until her skin felt tight and gritty. She remembered eating sweet, warm snap peas straight off the stalk, sucking on the ends of super-sour rhubarb stalks with her cousins, and carrying in baskets of fresh vegetables for that night's dinner. Those satisfying memories were punctuated by lemonade and bird calls, quiet companionship and blessed obscurity.

How had she managed to forget all that?

Each day, she waited impatiently on Gerri's terrace, eyes trained on the garden, her stomach quivery with excitement for the moment when Torien would arrive. Today was no different. Iris paced the sun-warmed stone floor, awaiting the sight of Torien rounding the cottage from where she usually parked her old white pickup truck. Half an hour passed, then an hour. Two. No luck.

This skin-tingling sense of anticipation for the arrival of another person was an old memory she had buried. When her ex, Melody, the drummer for a platinum-selling indie rock band, dumped her for some wide-eyed groupie, Iris had consciously numbed her romantic side. Never mind that Melody never looked back. Never mind that she and Iris hadn't shared the kind of love that lasted a lifetime. Never mind the sobering fact that Iris had known, deep inside, she and Mel were an ill-matched pair from the beginning. Bottom line? Iris had opened herself up emotionally. And for all that risk, she not only got *dumped*, but also blown through the ensuing media shitstorm on the fire-breath of the ravenous paparazzi dragon. The tabloids ridiculed her relationship and minimized her pain, as if "getting over it" should be no big deal for a supermodel. As if she had no real human emotions—didn't even deserve to. And that made her strive for just that—*not* to have any real human emotions.

So much safer to be closed off from life.

Months after the breakup, once the dragon had run out of fire and tabloid focus moved on to another story, Iris had thrown herself into her work and forbade anyone to mention Melody's name in her presence. She'd begun to "show up and look pretty," just as all her handlers had urged her to do from day one of her career. She swore off dating—at least within the semi-public circle of her friends and management—having reached her lifetime limit of being snagged by users and climbers who saw her as a commodity rather than a woman with dreams and feelings and worries of her own.

So she couldn't quite shake her astonishment over the fact that a certain strong, silent gardener had broken through her defenses in such a short time. That fluttery, floppy, can't-take-a-breath feeling assailed her, and she wound her arms around her abdomen. Torien never made her feel like an object—to the extreme sometimes, she thought ruefully. But each time Iris worried that, perhaps, Tori didn't find her the least bit attractive, Iris would remember the way she'd watched her from the door of the potting shed…and she knew.

She knew.

Torien was as attuned to her as she was to Torien, but something stood in the way. She meant to find out what that obstacle was. Soon. The days were rushing past, and she had a little less than a month before she left for Paris.

She scanned the gardens again. Damn, where was she?

Disappointment pulled a sigh from her lungs, and she decided to get started without Torien. The distinct possibility existed that Torien had a day off. God knew Iris hadn't seen her take one yet. And Tori deserved it. But that didn't mean Iris couldn't get in a little gardening herself.

She quickly changed into fitted yoga shorts and a racerback tank, then clipped her iPod into her waistband and situated the buds in her ears. She was pathetically behind in her reading, and she'd downloaded a lesbian mystery she'd missed and had been dying to read. It would be a good substitute companion while she worked. Trooping down to the garden, she chose the kidney-shaped bed of grape hyacinth and began to weed, just like Torien had taught her.

Half an hour passed, and Iris fell into a steady working rhythm. She twisted her hand, wrapping long grassy weeds around her palm, and tugged. The solid, ripping sensation as the earth relinquished the roots gratified her unlike anything she'd done in a long time. One task…one simple, repetitive task…so satisfying. She would have to remember this the next time she wanted to yank Geraline's head off. Her lips quirked.

She finished the grape hyacinth section and stood back to scrutinize her work, absorbing the expanse of accomplishment through her chest. Every finished task, no matter how tiny, felt like a step toward some amorphous "better." Calmness settled over her. Had she realized the therapeutic benefits of gardening, she'd have been out here long ago. The soil smelled rich and somehow secretive, dark and deeply moist. A balmy breeze sluiced along her skin and ruffled her hair. This recent partnership she'd forged with the earth was a purely elemental, purely simple, purely spiritual connection. Something she hadn't had, and clearly needed.

A warm, rough hand on her shoulder startled her. She gasped, spinning to find Torien behind her. Tucking a finger in the cords holding her earbuds in place, she tugged them out and let them dangle. "Crap. You scared me. Again." She reached down and pressed the stop button on her iPod, then smiled up at Torien as the thrill of seeing her lifted her spirits. Her smile quickly faded when she recognized the tight, blazing look of anger on those gorgeous features.

"What are you doing?"

Iris stilled for a moment, then aimed a thumb over her shoulder at the tidy flower bed, her throat tightening like a child busted for lighting matches under the wooden deck. "I just thought I would get started on some weeding until you got here. I'm sorry if I overstepped my bounds. I should've asked…I guess?"

"I did not mean to—" Torien stepped back, hands low on her hips, arms loose. She hung her head and shook it, then implored Iris. "I sounded harsh. *Lo siento*. I do appreciate all you have done to help…"

Iris crossed her arms, a punch of nausea stealing her breath. She had annoyed Torien, when all she hoped for was a gleam of approval in those dark, serious eyes. Now Torien was going to tell her she couldn't work in the gardens anymore. Iris could feel it, along with that deep heartbeat pounding against her back ribs. "But?"

"But...it doesn't look good."

Surprise riddling through her, Iris whipped a dismayed glance over her shoulder at the flower bed, wondering if she'd accidentally pulled up plants instead of weeds.

"Not that, sweet Irisíta. The flower bed looks perfect."

"Oh. Then...what—?"

Torien's expression mixed equal parts apology and worry. "I know she's not here, but if *Señora* Moreno saw you, her *guest*, doing my work, she would fire me."

Understanding dawned, and Iris felt sicker yet. She pressed her palms together and raised them to her lips. "I didn't even think. But—" Torien worked harder than any woman she had ever seen. She arrived at work each afternoon looking as if she'd already put in a full day of physical labor. Iris knew Geraline, though. Image, image, image. To her, it wouldn't matter.

Torien was dead-center correct.

She reached out and tentatively touched Torien's muscle-corded forearm. "I'm so sorry. I didn't stop to consider...it's just, I've so enjoyed working out here. God...I didn't mean to put you in a bad position, Torien. Please know that."

"Of course." Torien's expression relaxed in slow degrees. "Perhaps you will agree to work in the garden only when I am working, no? When I'm not, you just relax here. Read. Enjoy the flowers and the new growth. Be a guest."

Such a reasonable woman. Iris smiled, but she sort of wanted to cry. Weird. "Absolutely. Thank you for understanding."

The moment passed as quickly as it had arisen, morphing into something deeper, more languid, but at the same time more urgent. Desire licked up inside Iris. It felt as if the gardens were theirs alone, and no one existed outside the bubble of their entwined gazes.

Torien broke the spell with an almost imperceptible shake of her head and a long, slow exhale. "Still up for a little work?" Her callused thumb caressed a piece of dirt from Iris's cheekbone, ever so gently.

The simple touch felt more intimate to Iris than sex, sending a spray of shivers across her nerve endings. Her breathing had shallowed to the point that any words she uttered would telegraph her need. So…she nodded.

"Let's get to it, then," Torien said in a velvety tone.

Two hours passed as quickly as dandelion seed blowing on the wind. Iris welcomed the silence working alongside Torien, who never spoke when there wasn't something important to say, Iris had quickly learned. Torien's wasn't an angry silence. More a soul-deep respect for the work, a reverence for the earth and nature's soundtrack around them. A companionable, comfortable, physical quiet.

The sunset transformed the sky into a blanket of gilt-edged indigo, and their earlier discussion faded to a distant memory, much to Iris's relief. A staccato glance showed Torien engrossed in her work, her deft hands in the earth, working magic. Iris cleared her throat, the sound louder than she'd intended, and Torien's gaze came up.

"Ready to quit?"

"Not me," Iris said. "I'd be out here all night if I could."

Torien laughed short and shook her head with regret. "I probably will be. I am behind in my work."

The perfect opening. She straightened her back for a quick break and rested her hands in her lap. "Do you work another job? Is that why you're usually here in the afternoons?"

Torien pressed her lips together. Weighing…always weighing how much she should share, what might be crossing a line. At last, she nodded, standing and brushing her palms on the well-worn thighs of her jeans. She held up a *be right back* finger.

Iris watched Torien disappear into the tool shed, and when she returned with a bag of fertilizer on her shoulder, she said, "I work with a project…" She seemed to struggle with her words. "Not like a paid job. How do you say—?"

"Volunteer work?"

"Ah, yes. So very much the same word. *Voluntario.*" She bent her knees slightly and heaved the fertilizer bag onto the ground. "We are building community gardens in neighborhoods where there is not much beauty such as this. So the people have a place to relax." Torien flipped a hand to encompass their surroundings. "To do what we are doing."

"I think I've heard of that group." Iris tucked her hair behind her ears. "What's it called?"

"El Proyecto de Arco Iris."

"That's right. The Rainbow Project." A small, grassroots effort. Very effective, however, which was why it had garnered so much local press. "There was quite a write-up in the papers a while back."

Torien cocked her head to the side, pulled a clip knife from her pocket, flipped it open, and sliced open the plant food bag.

"About how the community—I can't remember which one—pulled together to improve the quality of life." She sat back on her haunches and watched while Torien filled a spreader with pungent, dark contents of the bag. She tried not to focus on the bunch and flex of Torien's arm muscles, though it was difficult. Now wasn't the time to cruise Torien's bod.

"We are a small group, all volunteer, but it's a worthwhile mission, *sí*. We wish there could be more worksites instead of one at a time, but that takes many hands." Torien set the half-full bag back on the ground and shrugged. "Madeira and I work together, but we must both hold other jobs to pay the bills. The way of life, no?" She jerked her head, indicating Iris should follow her if she desired. They crossed to the back of the gardens where a grassy expanse lay hidden from the mansion behind a half-circle of lilac bushes.

"Wow. It's gorgeous back here." Iris spun in a small, slow circle, taking it all in. "I didn't even know about this."

"A secret garden." Torien led Iris to a small bench. "Take a break, if you wish, while I do this."

Iris settled in, watching Torien snake back and forth across the expanse of lawn. The fertilizer whirled from the bottom of the spreader, hitting the perfect green grass blades before sinking to the soil beneath. On Torien's third pass, Iris sighed and stood. "I'm not in the mood to just sit. Mind if I walk with you?"

Ever stoic, ever polite, Torien appeared puzzled. "If you wish."

Iris ambled alongside, arms crossed, enjoying the bird calls and the wind through the leaves and thinking about what Torien had told her. So that was where she spent her days. Volunteering what little free time she had, unmindful of how physically draining it was. What a different type of person Torien was from other women she had known. Melody, the musician ex, had once thrown a tantrum over a recording contract that was half a million dollars below what she'd expected. Iris had been taken aback then, but now, disgust overwhelmed her. Mel hadn't donated a single moment of her precious time unless it guaranteed her coverage in the tabloids.

Iris studied Torien's angled profile, fighting the urge to brush away the perspiration trickling down her temple. What kind of life did she believe Iris lived? Did Torien imagine *she* would complain over a five-hundred-thousand-dollar discrepancy in pay? A nagging hand of shame about her good fortune clawed at Iris's conscience. She had earned her money, sure. But mostly because she'd inherited good genes and had seized the modeling opportunities that had come her way. She frowned. Wait a minute—why did she suddenly feel the need to defend herself? She wasn't Antoine, after all. Mr. Entitlement.

"Where is *El Proyecto* working now?" Iris asked, yearning to know more about this intriguing woman instead of wallowing in the unsettling and uncharacteristic guilt for her own comparatively easy life. "I read online that you'd finished that garden on the West End."

Torien made an affirmative sound low in her throat, eyes focused on her task. "We are in my neighborhood now. Círculo de Esperanza, on the north side."

Circle of Hope. Iris knew of it, yes. A modest immigrant

neighborhood referred to derisively by many Denverites as Tortilla Flats, due to the large population of Mexicans who lived there. Having grown up in the suburbs, she was ashamed to admit she'd never really been to Torien's neighborhood, though it wasn't so far from where they stood now. "Is there room for a community garden near your home?"

"*Sí*. Directly in front of our home, *en realidad*." At Iris's look of confusion, she added, "Our house sits on the corner of a square." Torien lifted one hand off the handle of the spreader and drew a shape in the air. "The square was empty. *Feo*, no?"

"Ugly?"

"Yes." Torien smiled. "But we'll make it beautiful."

Warmth radiated from within Iris. How appropriate that Torien should live in a place called Circle of Hope. "You live there with your sister?"

"And two other *compañeros*. Do you say...roommates?"

"Yes."

Torien shot her an almost embarrassed glance. "When we first arrived from *México*, we could not afford a place alone." She shrugged. "Now we are...used to each other, I suppose. They are all hardworking women. Decent."

Iris didn't doubt that.

"*A propósito*"—Torien ventured—"*Señora* Moreno has allowed me to borrow equipment for the community project. If you see me taking it...that is why."

Stopping short, Iris faced Torien. Clearly, she feared being accused of theft. Did she really think the possibility would cross Iris's mind? "Torien, you don't have to explain yourself to me. I would never doubt your integrity."

Torien pressed her lips together. "I meant no offense. I live in a different world, one where you can't be too careful. I thought I would mention it. Just in case."

Iris's jaw tightened and her mind raged. It shouldn't have to *be* that way. A pang of compassion clenched her stomach, and she reached out to touch Torien's lean, strong back, intended as a gesture of understanding. However, the feel of the cotton clinging lightly to the sweat-dampened muscles beneath mesmerized Iris, and, God help her, she couldn't make herself stop. She smoothed her hand up, then down again, feeling Torien tense beneath the caress. Still, Iris didn't pull away.

Finally, Torien stilled. Glanced at her, as if trying to puzzle it out. Iris recognized the smoldering look in Torien's eyes, the promise and the need of it, because she felt it herself.

She eased closer, yearning for Torien's touch. Craving confirmation that Torien felt this crackling sensation stretched taut between them, too. That Iris wasn't the only one consumed by it. Instead, Torien reached behind her and gently captured Iris's wrist, removed it from her back. Holding it loosely in her hand, Torien massaged Iris's pulse point with gentle motions of her work-roughened thumb. "We cannot." Torien's words were low, intimate. "You know this as well as I do." Her sobered, unwavering gaze searched Iris's face.

"Why not?" Iris whispered.

"Too many complications." Torien moistened her lips with a flick of her tongue. *"Si esta víbora te pica, no hay remedio en la botica.* You understand?"

Iris tried to translate in her head. Something about a snake bite with no remedy to cure the poison, the subtext of which wasn't sinking in. "I…uh…haven't heard that one."

"In English, you might say…playing with fire, no?"

"Ah, I see. But I don't understand why you think so." Iris inched closer until she could feel the heat radiating off Torien's body. "Is it me?"

"Yes," Torien replied, with a small huff of humorless laughter. Honest as always.

The answer surprised Iris, but it shouldn't have.

"It is you. And me." Torien released Iris's wrist and stepped back, motioning across the distance between them. "And all this. All that separates us."

"What separates us, Tori, except you? Your worry?"

Torien's jaw clenched. She flickered her eyes closed, then open again. "Don't do this."

"Why not? Don't you want to explore this...this *thing* between us?" Iris asked, feeling brazen. Wanting answers. "You feel it, too. I know you do because I see it in your eyes." Her heart beat hummingbird wings against her rib cage. Torien was shutting her out before they ever had a chance, and a small, pathetic part of Iris felt desperate to change her mind.

After several frozen moments, Torien leaned a palm on the handle of the spreader. One side of her mouth lifted in a sad half-smile. "I feel it. But what I want and what I must do are often two different things."

"Meaning?"

Torien released a long breath through her nose and smoothed the backs of her fingers along Iris's collarbone. "Ah, Irisíta. There are a million reasons why we cannot spend that kind of time together. I don't even have the words to list them all."

Iris's stomach plunged with humiliation and regret. "B-but we're spending time together right now." She lifted her arms to the sides. "What do you call this?"

"This is different."

"How so?" *Why so affronted?* a voice inside Iris chided. *You assume any woman would fall at your feet because you're* Iris Lujan? She didn't; that wasn't her vibe. But...Jesus.

Maybe she wasn't Torien's type.

Maybe this was her way of letting Iris down easy. She should accept it with dignity, no matter how difficult that was to dredge up. Iris held up a hand. "You know what? Don't answer. I just—" She paused, fighting to leach the raw emotion from her voice. She was a grown woman. She'd handled worse than a simple "thanks, but no thanks."

"*¿Qué?*" Torien tucked her chin and lifted Iris's slightly with a knuckle.

"What I mean is...we seem to get along well."

Torien inclined her head. "Very well."

Iris flipped her hands, defeated. Embarrassed. *Last kid picked for kickball.* "Well, then, I guess I just don't understand."

"Don't you?" The question sounded gently skeptical. Torien pointed toward the mansion where Iris was a guest, where *she* worked as the gardener. "We live in completely different worlds. Worlds so far apart it is...*increíble* that our paths even crossed. Nothing is ever going to change that."

Torien had a point. Still, Iris blinked at the woman who'd somehow managed to invade her thoughts and get under her skin in a way she hadn't experienced...maybe ever. She lowered her voice to a near whisper. "I get that. But...does it matter?"

Torien stared at her for a long time, then sighed, looking both regretful and fully reconciled to her decision. She danced her fingertips over Iris's cheek, down her neck to her shoulder, then squeezed her arm before breaking the connection completely. "I'm sorry, but this is real life. It matters a lot."

CHAPTER FOUR

Y o!" Emie snapped her fingers twice. "Earth to Iris, come in, Iris."

Startled, Iris blinked twice and refocused on her two best friends across the dimly lit restaurant table. Caught daydreaming—how embarrassing. She'd been doing that a lot in the past couple of weeks, more so since yesterday's cutting rejection. "I'm sorry." She closed her eyes and shook it off. "What did you say?"

Emie Jaramillo and Paloma Vargas exchanged a quick, cryptic glance. Paloma covered Iris's hand with her own. "Girl, if you were any more out of it, we'd put your ass in a home."

"Locked down," Emie added.

"Yeah," Paloma said, with a fleeting smile. "What's going on with you?"

Whenever Iris was in town, going out to lunch was their weekly ritual. Since it hadn't happened nearly often enough in the past few years, she cherished these moments. She shouldn't sit here ignoring the two people who had *never* rejected her— even on that fateful camping trip when she'd been sprayed by a skunk—just because Torien had. Indecipherable emotions swung like a wrecking ball in her stomach. "Eat first, then talk," she said, pasting a falsely bright smile on her face.

They returned frequently to this particular burger joint because no one seemed to recognize Iris, and if someone did, there might be discreet gawking, but no one disrupted their meal. The three of them would sit in a dark, high-backed booth for at least three hours, catching up on all the gossip while indulging in artery-clogging food and umbrella drinks until they had to unfasten the top buttons of their pants just so they could breathe.

For the next several moments, they sat buried in their familiar, oversized menus, exclaiming over the new dishes and arguing over whether margaritas were best frozen or on the rocks. Piped-in alternative music muffled the conversations around them, and the scents of grilled beef and fried vegetables permeated the air. As the menu offerings blurred before Iris's eyes, the question resurfaced. *Why doesn't she want me?*

She had seen evidence of their mutual physical attraction in Torien's eyes, felt it crackling like lightning in the air around them. She didn't think Torien had a girlfriend, or she probably would have mentioned it. Plus, she didn't seem the type of woman to keep such secrets. It had to be the other reason, the one she didn't want to think about. Perhaps a woman like Iris, occupying such a superficial place in the world, held no interest for a woman like Tori, who was so clearly grounded and self-assured. How could Iris prove there was more to her than pouting for the camera when, lately, she hardly believed it herself? She bit her lip, desperately needing the advice and support of her friends, but she would wait until they'd at least shared the traditional basket of fried mozzarella sticks and ranch dressing.

Then she'd spill her guts.

They ordered, dabbled in a little small talk, and soon the cheese sticks and margaritas—two on the rocks, one frozen— arrived.

Paloma, who at a diminutive four foot eleven always had trouble with the tables being too tall, slipped her foot beneath her like a booster chair. She reached across the dark oak table for a cheese stick, emitting a low yummy sound. "Nothing like fat, deep-fried in fat, dipped into more fat to launch the perfect best friends' luncheon."

Emie laughed. "Wouldn't be the same without them."

They both watched Iris, who usually pounced on the appetizer. When they'd each reached for their second stick before she'd lifted a hand, Emie sighed. "Okay, Iris. Forget this 'let's eat first' stalling. You aren't eating anyway."

"Yes, I am."

"No," Paloma said. "You aren't."

Emie pinned her with a level gaze. "What's going on?"

Iris reached for a cheese stick in a small, pathetic sign of rebellion. After dunking it in the dressing, biting into it, chewing, and swallowing, she took a long sip of her cocktail, then said, "Okay, fine." A beat passed. "I met a really great woman."

"What?" Paloma shrieked. "And you were going to make us wait for that story? It's red ink for you tonight, Iris."

Her tiny friend scowled, and Iris laughed. Paloma had kept extensive journals since they were kids. When she wrote about you in *red ink*, you were number one on her shit list.

"Whatever happened to that 'if I need to snuggle, I'll get a dog' mantra you've been chiming since Mel took off with the groupie?" Emie asked.

Iris groaned, pulling the turquoise paper umbrella out of her drink and sucking foam off the end of the toothpick. "Well, I guess *she* happened."

"Who?" Paloma said.

"This...incredible woman she met," Emie answered, glancing to Iris for confirmation. "Right?"

Iris nodded.

"So? Not a good enough answer. Who is she?" Emie asked.

A tight pause ensued while Iris imagined their reactions. "Geraline's new gardener." She watched their faces, which remained open but inscrutable. They'd made a pact in high school to reserve judgment on any potential dates until they'd heard the whole story. Twelve years since they'd graduated, and the pact still held. Iris smiled, feeling suddenly cocooned in the solidarity of their...forever-ness.

"Her name is Torien Pacias. She's Mexican—"

"News flash: so are we," Paloma said.

"I mean from Mexico Mexican. Like Emie's parents."

Emie smiled.

"Anyway, she's here on a permanent work visa. She's tall—"

"Tall?" they asked in unison, knowing that Iris was usually the tall one in her relationships.

"Yep. Tall, dark, and drop-dead...just...I don't know. Freaking *hot*. Not to mention, sweet. But not too sweet, if you know what I mean. Always kind and caring enough to make you want to rip your clothes off and beg, but she's definitely got a sexy brood to her, too. Without all that moody baggage stuff that often goes with the dark, sexy, brooding type, thank God."

"So, basically perfect," Paloma said.

"Yep." Iris fidgeted into a more comfortable position, then looked from woman to woman. "So?"

"What do you mean, 'so'? What else?" Paloma asked, wrapping her hand around the base of her gargantuan margarita glass. "If you met a great woman, end of story, your expression wouldn't look like someone drop-kicked your kitten into its tenth life."

Iris released a little huff of astonishment and glanced at Emie for support.

Emie shrugged. "Sorry. Pea has a point."

"Okay, you're right. This time it's not so easy as, met a woman who personifies perfection, cue romantic music—"

"Is it ever?" Emie asked.

Iris scoffed. "Only for Paloma." She quickly explained how they met, that they'd been gardening together, and all about Torien's volunteer work. Then she twisted her lips into a derisive grimace and added, "There's only one problem."

"Problem? What?" Emie asked, nudging her glasses up the bridge of her nose. "She sounds great so far."

"She *is* great. The most amazing, real, honest woman I've

ever met." Iris sat back, her gaze on the table, fingers twirling the paper umbrella. "Alas, she doesn't want me."

"Ah. So, she's straight?" Paloma said, not missing a beat. Emie smacked her, and Paloma scowled. "What?" She indicated their famous friend across the table. "She's Iris Lujan, for God's sake. If the woman isn't interested in *her*, gardener chick's either dead-set heterosexual, or she's got the kind of baggage I don't *even* want to open."

"Paloma, be serious. I'm not interested in women who want to date *Iris Lujan*"—Iris bracketed the statement with finger quotes—"and you damn well know that. I want a woman who wants *me*. The real me. The me you guys know. Actually…to be more specific, I want *Torien* to want that me. But it's just…not happening."

Paloma pursed her lips and took hold of Iris's other hand. "We do understand, honey. I didn't mean to be flippant."

Iris glanced down to stanch the raw sting of impending tears, and her tone lowered. "I want this more than anything I've wanted in a long time. I don't know what to do."

They paused while the waitress served their entrees, and when she left, Emie asked, "How can you be so sure Torien's not interested?"

Worried what the food might do to her churning stomach, Iris pushed her plate away. "Because she told me."

Emie blinked, startled. "Just…straight out?"

"Pretty much." She made a shooing motion with her hands. "Go ahead and eat. Don't wait for me." She waited for them to settle the jade cloth napkins on their laps and dig forks into their respective entrées before asking, "Okay"—she sighed—"where should I start with the whole 'she doesn't want me' tale of woe?"

"Tell all," Emie said, steak knife in her hand. "We'll ferret out the good parts."

Iris brought them up to speed with everything that had happened the previous evening. With a shrug, she added, "That's it. The woman isn't interested in dating me. She and her little sister are supporting their family in Mexico, and I guess that takes up all her time. I don't know."

"Does she know who you are?" Emie eyed her. "Is she intimidated?"

"Uh, trust me. Torien isn't intimidated by anything. She knows about my job but doesn't seem to care." Iris unfurled her cloth napkin and listlessly extracted the fork. She bounced it against her hand beneath the table. "That's one of the main reasons I like being around her so much."

"Because she accepts you," Paloma said.

"That, and she doesn't treat me…differently."

"Probably because, as a foreigner, she understands what it feels like to be a loner amongst many," Emie murmured.

Iris's gaze jerked toward her. How'd Em get to be so smart? Well, besides that decade-plus she spent in college and grad school. Emie, a renowned research scientist, never failed to analyze situations in the most logical manner. And, as usual, she had an astute point. Being well-known and recognizable kept Iris more isolated than she preferred. Torien seemed kind of isolated, too. So, why couldn't they isolate themselves together and do what nature intended? "It *does* feel like she gets me, you know? If I could just—"

"What does she like to do?" Paloma interjected.

Iris's forehead crinkled. "Huh?"

"Hobbies, interests. Find out what she likes to do and ask to join her. Better yet, join her without asking. That's usually your M.O., right? Maybe she just doesn't feel comfortable enough to do all the planning at this stage."

Iris rolled her eyes. "Yeah, that would seem natural. 'Torien, I heard you were into stamp collecting and, well, I just happened to be in the post office…'"

"Okay, true. Too contrived," Paloma conceded.

"Besides, I've been working in the garden with her." Iris didn't want to force herself on Torien any more than she already had. "I've made it abundantly clear I'm interested...in not so many words." Her skin flushed. Actually, in *exactly* those words.

"Slow your roll, sister. You came on to her?" Paloma rasped, leaning forward until the lamp light shone on her auburn hair.

Chagrined, Iris said, "Ah, I...I guess I did."

Paloma clicked her tongue. "Iris, darlin', take a lesson from babies, girl. You gotta crawl before you walk. Pull back and be her friend before you jump her gorgeous bones. She'll come around eventually, guaranteed. What's not to like about you? And I'm *not* referring to your career, fame, money, success, freakish beauty—"

"I get it," Iris said, with a soft laugh. She smiled across the table at her friends, warm in the circle of their caring. Her chin quivered and she bit her lip. "You really think that'll do it? I don't have much time before I leave for my assignment."

"Yes!" Paloma exclaimed, just as Emie added, "Of course!"

The three of them laughed at their all-too-familiar habit of talking over each other, then Emie said, "If you really like this woman, then take the chance. If it works out, it will be worth it." She spread her left hand flat on the table and smiled down at the shiny new commitment ring nestled on her third finger. "Take it from me."

All three friends stared down at the ring on Emie's slim finger. Her nails were manicured short and buffed to a smart, natural patina. Paloma, who had been more married for the past twelve years than any stupid legal document could assert, placed her hardworking hand alongside Emie's, comparing the mellowed shine of her own ring. Iris placed her ringless, flawless, short French-manicured—despite all the recent gardening—hand fingertip-to-fingertip with them and realized just how much hands said about a person. She pulled away first, not thrilled with the message hers conveyed.

Soft, pampered, *empty*.

Maybe that was the real reason Torien showed zero interest in her. And yet, Iris wasn't *that* woman. Soft, pampered, empty.

Was she? She pressed her lips into a grim line, rattled by the realization that she wasn't sure of the answer, but determined to prove to Torien—and herself—it wasn't true.

❖

"Torien? *Toro!*"

A loosely packed wad of *tierra jardín* smacked Torien in the side of the face and crumbled, some of the dirt cascading down the back of her neck inside her collar. Torien spun toward Madeira's straight-from-the-belly laughter, simultaneously shaking the dirt out of her shirt and brushing it from her neck and ear. "What the hell are you doing?" she growled.

"Trying to get your attention, you bullheaded woman, like I've been doing for the past five minutes. You're a million miles away." Madeira spread her sculpted, deeply tanned arms and, for emphasis, she glanced around the field, freshly tilled for their newest community garden. "Life goes on around you, *hermana*. Have a look before you miss it." Madeira grinned, giving a small jerk of her chin. *"¿Qué mosca te ha picado?"*

"*Nada*, Mosquito," Torien said, but the corners of her lips lifted grudgingly. "We have a lot of work to finish, if you have not noticed." She could never stay angry at her charmer of a sister, especially when Madeira had a valid point. Indeed, all around them, women and men laughed and worked. A jet left a fluffy white trail in the rich turquoise sky above. Car horns tooted, sparrows chirped, hot cumbia rhythms thumped down from a nearby window. Yet all of it had faded while she stood there like a statue in the middle of the work site, her thoughts consumed by Iris and their difficult conversation in Moreno's garden.

Not that she'd admit that to Madeira.

She wasn't up for the jeers and innuendos. In truth, she had not told anyone, not even Madeira, that she had even met the superstar. Frankly, she could think of no good reason to do so. It wasn't as if Iris would ever come into contact with her family and friends. She rolled tension out of one shoulder, then the other. She merely indulged Iris's desire to garden because it was the polite thing to do for a guest of *la patrona*. There was nothing to her relationship with Iris beyond that. Well, friendship. And perhaps a sting of awareness, which was quite normal for healthy young women. But it didn't mean anything. *Who are you trying to convince, Toro?*

Quieting her conscience, she let herself picture Iris with the sun on her back and determination in the set of her jaw. Pride swelled in Torien's chest. For a soft, *mujeril* woman, Iris worked impressively hard. Torien could close her eyes and see the perspiration traveling from her neck down her chest, carving small trails through the dirt clinging there. Her lips twitched into a private smile at the image. Iris somehow managed to get dirt everywhere, even when she only pulled weeds. Her face, her chest, the top of her head. Torien never saw Iris turning somersaults through the soil but couldn't figure any other way she'd get so dirty.

"That spaced-out grin has 'lovestruck fool' written all over it," Madeira drawled, planting her fists on her hips. "You got something to tell your sister?"

Torien's stomach contracted as if Madeira had punched her. "Lovestruck? Don't be ridiculous." Her annoyed glare shot to Madeira, shorter than Torien by four inches but more muscular by half. Her good-looking sister had always had a way with the ladies, but Torien? Not so much. She was too stern, too serious, too...unlike Madeira...for most women. Lovesick? *¡Ay!* Mosquito had lost her mind if she believed it.

Torien gulped past a throat tightened with guilt.

Hijole madre. Am I that transparent?

Torien yanked up the handles of a wheelbarrow, avoiding Madeira's narrowed scrutiny and her own inner turmoil, and pushed it over the uneven surface of the dirt with jerky motions. "I've been working too hard to collect women or secrets," she tossed over her shoulder. "You should try doing the same."

"Being a smart young player, I make time for both." Madeira untied the bandanna she wore around her neck and mopped her forehead. "If you cannot have women or secrets, what's the point of living? I've been trying to tell you that, Toro, since puberty."

Long before that, Torien mused. She stopped to load jagged pieces of concrete they'd unearthed into the wheelbarrow and cast a feigned crabby glance at Madeira. "And I've been trying to tell you life is about more than making love and killing *cervezas* for just as long."

"Once you prove it to me, I'll stop. Until then"—Madeira winked—"too many ladies, too little time, no?"

Torien snorted. "Someday you are going to pass up the right woman in your rush to get to the next one."

"I'll believe that old wives' tale when it happens." Madeira crossed over to help with the concrete. "Until then, I'm testing the waters."

A little flash of admiration struck Torien, and she ducked her face to hide her smile. At twenty-four, Madeira was seven years younger than she. But sometimes Torien thought her sister had grasped the nuances of living life to the fullest straight out of the womb. She envied Madeira her zest, daring, and outgoing— even audacious—personality, but those were traits and privileges reserved for the younger sister, she supposed. As eldest, Torien's familial responsibilities outweighed her desire to cut loose like Madeira, the quintessential life of the party. Torien raised her eyebrows and inclined her head. "Do what you must, but don't forget, I am older and smarter."

Madeira snorted. "Older is obvious. You talk like a white-haired *abuelita*." She waved at Torien in disgust. "Keep it up and I'm going to buy you a house dress to match your attitude."

"*¡Cállate!*"

"You always tell me to shut up when I hit a nerve. You're predictable as a lapdog. And about as interesting." Madeira puffed with pride as she studied Torien with renewed interest.

She narrowed her eyes and chewed on the inside of her cheeks. "Mmm-hmm, it's obvious."

Torien sighed. "What now?"

"Something is making your brain soft. Don't bother denying it." She knocked her fist against her chest. "I'm your *hermana*. I know you better than you know yourself. I'd bet you two cold *cervezas* it's a woman."

"I told you, there is no—"

"Relax. I understand your reluctance to tell me, Toro." Madeira flipped her palms forward and turned her head to the side, playing at nonchalance. "You are afraid to bring the lady around the *ladróna de corazones*." She flared her nostrils with mock arrogance and sniffed. "It is wise of you to worry that I might steal her heart. How could I fail?"

Torien laughed out loud. "Any woman I would be interested in wouldn't be fooled by your flexed muscles and flirting, *serpiente*. And I don't have time for a *cerveza* tonight, so you can keep your bet." She shook her head, unsure whether to smile at her sister or slug her. It had always been this way, since they were barefooted, tree-climbing girls.

"Okay, no woman. If you say so. But whatever is making you look so dreamy and eager, Toro, keep with it as long as it's legal." Madeira jerked her chin up. "*Oye*. Is it legal?"

Torien gave her the evil eye. "*¿Quién te mete, Juan Copete?*"

Madeira struggled for a look of innocence, her shoulders hiking in the manner of the unfairly accused. "Is it so wrong for me to wish my sister happiness?"

"Mosquito—"

"You take life too seriously." Madeira rapped her on the shoulder with the back of her knuckles and lowered her tone conspiratorially. "Take a lesson from your *hermanita*. I know lots of ladies who would be glad to break you out of your—"

"I get the picture, no? Not interested." Torien grabbed a

fistful of her sister's T-shirt and pulled her face closer. "And when the day comes that I need my baby sister's help with my love life, you'll be the first to know. Now, drop it and help me finish."

Amusement in her thickly lashed eyes, Madeira nodded slowly, straightening her wrinkled shirt with exaggerated motions, but respecting Torien's request. Whether joking or serious, that impenetrable bedrock of respect supported their relationship and kept them close.

For several minutes, they worked side by side, loading all the cracked concrete into the wheelbarrow and carting it to the battered Chevy pickup they used for trips to the dump. When they'd cleared the lot of debris, they sat for a moment on the tailgate of the truck, sharing Madeira's last Pepsi between them.

"Working for *la mujer rica* again tonight?"

"*Sí.*" Torien ran her hand through her hair acknowledging, for the first time, her bone-deep exhaustion, how utterly out of sorts she felt.

Partly, it was the long hours.

Partly, it was *her*. Iris…untouchable Iris.

"Every night. Between this job and that, I hardly have time to remember my name."

"But that one pays the bills."

"I know."

Madeira's forehead wrinkled with worry. "We need more help, Toro. I want this garden to be our most beautiful, considering"—she gestured toward a painted brick townhouse to their left—"it will be the view from our front window." She quirked her mouth. "I shouldn't play favorites."

"I understand. I feel the same." Torien gave Madeira a half-smile. "Octavia said she would bring more people next week. Natán is bringing his new wife, Judit, and her sister. I put an ad in the Spanish papers calling for volunteers, too. We'll make it work." A beat passed, sister to sister, so much being said without the hindrance of words. "Haven't we always?"

"Mmm. I just keep wondering when our luck will run out."

Torien drank deeply from the can, then handed it back. "Not until we give up. Moreno said I could borrow supplies from her *sotechado*, so that will help."

Madeira grunted in acknowledgment. "What does she have?"

Torien almost laughed at the question. "Everything. And more. As long as it stays in good condition, we can use it."

"*¡Bueno!* We'll start with it right away." Madeira regarded her sister with laser scrutiny. She whistled between her bottom teeth. "No offense, Toro, but you look like a mutt that's been tied to the back of a moving truck. *¡Qué lástima!* Forget what I said about you having a secret woman on the side. She'd have to be toothless and blind to want a *bruja vieja* like you."

Torien expelled a little amused gush of air. "I told you, I'm working hard. I don't have time to primp and pamper like you and your pretty friends."

Madeira laughed. "Speaking of *la pandilla*, last chance to tip a few back with us at the club. What do you say? It's obvious you need it."

"Can't. Too much to do at the estate." It wasn't the whole truth; she'd gotten a lot done this past week with Iris's help. But admitting that she just wanted to…be there would require an explanation about Iris, and Torien wasn't ready to share what little she allowed herself to have of her garden angel. Not with anyone. Not even with Madeira, the person she felt closest to in the world.

Torien didn't even know if Iris would return after what had happened last night. Stabbed with regret, she tried not to think about it and knew damn well she must keep the whole sordid mess to herself. No matter how she explained it, Madeira would blow everything out of proportion, embarrassing Torien as well as Iris. Nothing could come of this powerful attraction. Why make it worse by wrapping the futile situation in words?

"You've been putting in too many hours here. I can come by the estate to help if you'd like."

"No," Torien said, a bit too quickly. She cringed inwardly, knowing Madeira had caught the rapid response by the curious expression she wore. "You're too young to spend all your time working," Torien added, by way of explanation.

"That's the thing," Madeira said, in a rare serious moment. "So are you."

"Tell that to *mamá* and *las mellizas* when I don't earn enough to send one month. It's not just about me, Mosquito. I do not expect you to understand, but—"

"No worries." Madeira clapped a hand on Torien's shoulder. "Another time, then."

Torien gave a noncommittal nod.

Madeira offered the last bit of soda, but Torien waved it off.

As Madeira leaned her head back to drain the can, Torien added, "I plan to stay at Moreno's tonight, probably tomorrow to catch up on things, so you'll have the place to yourself." She paused for emphasis. "Don't make your little sisters lose respect, *serpiente*, or your *mamá* cry."

Madeira crushed the can in her palm, cocking a brow. "Should I give you the same admonition?"

Probing again. Torien favored her with a droll stare meant to show Madeira how well Toro knew her game. "Don't fool yourself into thinking that sharing a cold drink will make me want to swap love stories with the likes of you."

"You think that's why I shared the Pepsi?" Madeira exclaimed, trying to look hurt. Unfortunately, she couldn't hold back her amusement at having been caught in her ploy. "You insult me," she said, between the laughter.

"Sure I do." Torien shook her head with feigned disgust, a smile quivering the corners of her mouth. "Don't forget, you cannot fool the *hermana* who once diapered your bare brown ass."

Chapter Five

Much to Iris's surprise, Torien was already hard at work when she padded out to the terrace the next morning, a cup of steaming coffee in her hands. *Damn.* Painful talons of unsatiated desire gouged into her at the mere sight of Torien. She wondered briefly why Tori wasn't at her volunteer worksite that morning, as usual, but mostly she was excited to have her nearby.

They needed to talk.

Understatement.

Unfortunately, her chicken-hearted soul prevented her from simply walking downstairs to face Tori, woman to woman. Granted, Tori hadn't *said* Iris shouldn't come back to help in the garden, but Iris had decided it would be more comfortable to have Tori walk up on her rather than the opposite. After all, Iris was the one who'd been snubbed. She didn't think she could take it again.

She watched her from a semi-hidden spot on the terrace, biding her time. Finally, around noon, Torien threw her arms up in the air, then stalked away from a piece of equipment she'd been tinkering with for an hour. Iris watched her pull that tall, muscular frame into the cab of her truck and slam the door. The engine growled to life. Off to purchase parts, Iris assumed, since Torien hadn't put her tools up for the day, and the woman was nothing if not conscientious. Iris listened to the truck rumble away, and then leapt on the chance.

Heart pounding, she raced to her suite and pulled on her rattiest holey, cut-off sweatpants, red Chuck Taylor high-tops, and a faded, paint-stained black T-shirt that read: EARTH IS FULL. GO HOME. She wound her hair into a messy wad and secured it with a couple of clips, then pummeled her way down the stairs, out the door, and into the garden. She hoped for a few solitary moments to school her features into a mask of nonchalance before Torien returned.

She knew she'd promised to work in the garden *only* when Torien was there…but she had a decent argument for believing she'd be right back. As Iris set about weeding a bed of multicolored lupine and soft blue perennial flax, she wondered what her next step would be. She hadn't thought that far ahead, and only hoped her ratty, careless attire would convey the message that Iris Lujan was no soft, pampered, *empty* slouch. She wanted Torien to know she had no problem whatsoever looking like crap and toiling in the dirt with the best of them. And liking it.

No more than fifteen minutes later, tires crunched over the gravel drive that wound to the back of the gardener's cottage, and a big truck came to a stop. The metallic groan of the door opening, then closing, and the uneven ticking of the hot engine revved her heartbeat to full throttle. Moment of truth. Torien could very well tell her to get lost, and that would be that. Or…not. Either way, Iris had to know.

Today.

Now.

Oh, God…what am I thinking?

She continued methodically weeding the flower bed, determined to act casual despite the fact she couldn't feel her extremities for the shower of nerve tingles. Her motions were jerky and her chest trembled with every inhale.

Footsteps approached, and it took every ounce of her

willpower not to turn toward Torien with some pathetic "please like me" expression she knew would show on her face like a fresh tattoo. Glancing down, she noticed her pulse thrumming beneath the skin of her wrist. Damn. It had been a long time since a woman affected her like this.

Please let this work, her mind whispered.

"Toro!" came a rich, smooth voice behind her. "You here?"

Startled, Iris shot to her feet and spun, automatically brushing the dirt from her palms. The young woman rounding the corner of the cottage froze, and her jaw dropped.

Her sculpted shoulders and lats tapered to a honed waistline, making her ripped arm muscles stand out from her body in true bodybuilder fashion. She was shorter than Torien, but the family resemblance couldn't be denied. Where Torien looked rough-edged and untamed, like a dark wolf, this woman appeared polished and perfect, like a sleek, black Arabian—both beautiful in her own unabashedly perfect way.

"M-Madeira?" This definitely had to be the little sister who "needed a keeper," as Torien often muttered while she and Iris worked together in the garden. It only took one look at the confident, loose-limbed way this younger Pacias hottie moved, and Iris didn't doubt her identity for a second. From her strong jaw and dimpled cheeks, neatly styled sweep of black hair, and overblown sex appeal—yep. Torien had been dead-on about her little sis. Madeira was the kind of flirtatious, irresistible lesbian every mother warned about and every father despised. Iris smiled, thrilled by the unexpected meeting. "Hi."

"*Madre de Dios.*" Madeira's keys dropped from her palm. She crossed herself quickly, finishing off with a kiss to the index-finger edge of her knuckles. "I didn't realize prayers could be answered so literally."

Laughing at her quick wit and charming melodrama, Iris skirted around the bed of irises she and Torien had planted together and headed toward her unexpected visitor. "You just missed your sister, I'm afraid. She left a few minutes ago." She indicated the broken contraption near the tool shed. "I think that machine was getting the best of her. You're welcome to wait."

"I…I'm here to pick up some *equipo la patrona de Toro* said we could borrow," came the jumbled response. Madeira's long throat tightened visibly as she swallowed. She gestured toward Iris, the stiff movement of a person in shock. "You—you're Iris Lujan, no? Standing right here in front of me?"

"I am." She inclined her head, her ears radiating with warm embarrassment. Madeira's stammering, girlish awe was really very sweet. Iris held out her hand. "Very nice to meet you."

"Oh, no." Madeira raised her hands, robbery style, her eyes wide with mock horror. "If I touch you, I will never be able to wash my hand again."

Iris's breath caught. She stilled.

At that, Madeira winked and burst into an infectious laugh. She reached for Iris's hand, clasping it between both of hers and shaking it with gusto. "The pleasure is all mine, *Señora* Lujan, believe me. I could die right now and go to heaven a happy woman. Happier if I could have an hour to brag to my friends first."

"Oh, cut it out. Your sister was right about you." She grinned. "And please, call me Iris. *Señora* sounds so old—ugh." Madeira's gregarious enthusiasm set her immediately at ease. "Torien didn't mention you'd be stopping by." Though they hadn't actually spoken, Iris remembered, after the words had left her lips.

"Toro didn't know." Madeira shrugged, stooping to swipe up her key ring and stuff it into her back pocket. "She's been busy, working way too hard."

"No kidding."

"I figured she could use the help loading tools and equipment in the truck."

Made sense. "Well, I think she lined it all up over here by the shed."

"Sounds like my perfectionist sister," Madeira said, ruefully.

Iris smiled and shook her head. She beckoned Madeira with a cupped hand. "Let me show you."

"No way. Forget the equipment." Madeira scissored her arms. "Do I look crazy? What kind of woman would choose working over being alone with Iris Lujan?"

Your sister seems to. Disappointment drizzled over Iris, but she forced it away, determined to maintain as light a mood as Madeira seemed to do without effort. "Let's sit for a minute, then." She guided Madeira to a bench and they sat. "I've heard so much about you."

"I wish I could say the same, but my selfish sister has managed to keep you all to herself. That dog." Madeira punched one fist into the opposite palm, then flashed her dimpled grin.

So Torien hadn't even mentioned her. Iris quirked her mouth to the side, realizing she wasn't nearly as important to Torien as Torien had become to her. She had known it inside, but hearing it confirmed by Madeira felt like an unexpected slap.

Madeira settled in, resting one ankle on the opposite knee and extending an arm along the back of the bench. "I knew she had a bad case of woman on the mind, though, even if she chose not to tell me."

Iris's interest perked. "What do you mean?"

"Something has been muddling Toro's brain for"—she flashed an adoring smile—"how long have you two known each other?"

"About two weeks, I guess," Iris said.

"I knew it!" Madeira slapped the back of one hand against the palm of the other, then twirled her fingers beside her temple. "That's just about when Toro started getting stupid in the head. But I would never have guessed it was Iris Lujan making her *loco*. Not in real life, at least. Unbelievable."

"Oh, shush." Iris pushed on Madeira's solid shoulder,

flattered but not threatened in the way she'd been before, when fans hero-worshiped her. "She's just working too hard."

"Toro always works hard," Madeira countered. "This is different. Now I know why."

This young, vibrant flirt seemed like she could be Iris's own little sister, her manner gushy, yes, but respectful, too. So different from her proud, reserved *hermana*, Iris mused, her stomach tightening with a warm tug of desire at the mere thought of Torien.

Madeira leaned in, lowering her tone secretively. "Did Toro tell you she papered our bedroom walls with your magazine pictures? I was only a kid, but I still remember."

Soft surprise blew through Iris, like dry leaves carried on the wind. She arched her eyebrows and crossed her arms. "No, as a matter of fact, she didn't."

"It's true." Madeira pantomimed a papered wall. "Covered, floor to ceiling." She sucked in one side of her cheek. "We have always called Toro the big dreamer, but look where it got her. I guess I can learn a thing or two from my big sister after all." She squeezed her eyes shut and clasped her hands together in front of her well-toned chest.

"Shakira. *¡Plegue á Dios!* Bring me Shakira, I beg," Madeira chanted. She peeked through one squinted eyelid at Iris, gauging her response in the manner of a seasoned joker. The eye snapped shut again, her lips twitching with amusement. "Or Jessica Alba, Father, I'm not picky." Crossing herself again, Madeira opened her eyes, shoulders shaking with her rich chuckle.

Iris joined her in laughter, then shook her head, studying this younger, smaller, more lighthearted version of Torien. "You and your sister are so different. But I can definitely see a family resemblance."

Madeira framed her fingers around her face. "*Sí*, I got the looks and charm, no? And Toro got all the seriousness."

"I'm not even touching that one," Iris said wryly, lifting her palms as if in surrender. "Though I'll admit, your sister *is* pretty intense." She hadn't meant to let her emotions show, but either she had or Madeira was particularly astute.

"No. Tell me no. Did that fool sister of mine do something to you, Iris?" Madeira frowned. "Tell me. I will tear her apart, purely on principle."

"Don't do that." Iris slanted her glance away. "Tori didn't do anything. She's a wonderful, kind woman. It's just...we're friends, but—" *I hoped for more.*

Lame.

Iris pursed her lips and studied Madeira. If anyone could provide insight into the enigmatic woman who had stolen her thoughts, Madeira could. But Iris would have to lay her heart on the line first. Did she dare? Could she trust Madeira? Something told her she could. Deep breath in...and exhale. "This has to stay between you and me," she implored.

"Absolutely." A distinct gleam of mischief lit Madeira's eyes. "I love to have secrets to hold over my sister's head."

Iris shored her courage, then gave the abridged version of what had happened the other night in the garden, finishing with, "What do you think?"

"I think my sister is an idiot."

Iris couldn't help but chuckle. "You don't miss a beat." She sighed. "Is it me?"

"It's her," Madeira assured.

"Does Torien have a girlfriend? Is that it?"

"Toro? My all-business sister?" Madeira scoffed. "The woman works from dawn 'til dark and more. She hardly has time to share a beer with her sister, let alone to charm the ladies."

"God, she is so frustrating." Iris pounded her thighs once with her fists.

"The one and only Iris Lujan has a thing for Toro," Madeira murmured, mostly to herself, a wry smile on her lips. "Isn't that just how it goes? I spend time on my looks, my charm, my muscles, and what happens? My grouch of a sister draws the attention of a dream woman like you."

Iris hugged her arms around her torso, feeling cared for, special. Torien's sister just inspired closeness. "I may be interested in Torien, but she isn't interested in me. Not like that. She says our worlds are too different."

"They are, but so what? She hasn't been herself since she met you, Iris. Trust me, she is interested. She just has trouble letting herself go." Madeira spat a quick string of Spanish that Iris didn't quite catch. She'd been able to pick out the words for "stubborn" and "nun," however, and bit back a grin.

Madeira patted Iris's hand. "Let me tell you something about my thick-headed sister, *amada*. She is a good, honorable woman. The best woman I know. But she carries the weight of the world on her shoulders."

"That, I can see."

Madeira stared off into the distance as though visualizing the story in her mind. "Our *papá* died too early. Since then, Toro feels it is up to her to keep the world spinning for all of us. For everyone. She has always been that way. We have two little sisters—"

"Tori told me about them." She layered her other hand on top of Madeira's.

"*Sí*, and *Mamá*. Toro has always taken care of all of us, when I was a girl—even now. I help, of course, but it is really she who holds it all together," Madeira added, her show of sincere modesty adding a pleasant dimension to her jovial personality. "It was Toro, even before *Papá* died." Madeira pressed her lips in a line and shook her head. "Torien does our father proud, but you cannot tell her that. She refuses to give herself a break."

"But why?"

Madeira shrugged. "Just won't. It's as if she feels responsible for *Papá*'s death, though it makes little sense. Or, I don't know, she feels responsible for living her life exactly opposite of how he did to prove some kind of a point. *Papá* died in a factory accident. Toro wasn't even there. But she carries that weight everywhere." Madeira released a long, exhale through her nose, and her expression told Iris she had been through this with her sister before.

Her heart swelled. "Torien is a woman of principles. You can't fault her for that."

Madeira gave a grunt of agreement. "Too many principles for her own good, in my opinion. Principles heavy with guilt Toro shouldn't bear." She eyed Iris seriously for a minute, chewing on the inside of her cheek. "Let me ask you something. What do you want from Toro?"

"I just—" Iris swallowed. What did she want? Friendship? Romance? Sex? No. More, though admitting it even to herself was a shock. Torien was the kind of woman who made Iris want it all. The kind who made her picture commitments and forever and home, who made her think of family. Maybe even children, like Paloma and Deanne had. Maybe not. All she knew at this point was—she wanted Tori. "I like her. I want to know her. She…makes me feel good about myself."

Madeira dialed in, sizing up the situation. "Nothing would please me more than seeing *mi hermana* happy." A pause ensued. After a moment, she shifted her position until she faced Iris fully. "Listen, Torien is more than a sister to me, she's my best friend."

"I understand. I can see that."

"She deserves a woman like you."

Iris swallowed. But did *she* deserve a woman like Tori? Honorable, kind, caring? Grounded in herself, her work, her place in this world? That was the million-dollar question. She let her gaze flutter to the earth, her throat aching with worry and guilt. Tori's sister wanted her to be happy, but perhaps Iris wasn't the kind of woman who could bring joy into Torien's life. Maybe they should let Torien decide what she wanted. And yet…

Iris couldn't let it go that easily. Some self-protective part of her wanted to pull away, but she forced herself to meet Madeira's eyes. "What can I do? She won't listen to me."

"*Oye.*" Madeira whipped a glance over her shoulder, then bestowed a devious, conspiratorial look. "When will she be back?"

"I don't know." All at once, a sense of urgency quickened Iris's pulse. "Soon."

Madeira laid a hand on Iris's shoulder and pulled her closer. "Then listen quickly, so I can go before she finds out I was here." She knocked on her temple with her knuckles. "I am smart as well as gorgeous"—she winked, stripping the arrogance from the statement—"and I think I have an idea."

Lost in somber thoughts about Iris, Torien wouldn't have even raised her eyes from her fence-building task, but the increase in galvanized chatter caught her attention. She smeared sweat from her forehead with the crook of her elbow and followed their gazes, noting with mild interest the red Mercedes sports car that had purred to a stop at the north curb of the Círculo de Esperanza worksite. Standing slowly, she brushed her palms against the denim covering her thighs. It wasn't every day a car such as this came into their neighborhood.

"*¿Qué pasó, Toro?*" Madeira appeared beside her.

Torien hiked one shoulder. "*Yo no sé.*"

They moved closer just in time to see Iris emerge from the driver's seat, all loveliness and softness—pure class. Torien stumbled to a stop, as did most of the other laborers. But after a single, silent, shock-riddled moment, the group erupted in pandemonium and excitement. Everyone moved about except Torien, who could not. Around her, exclamations in Spanish and English ensued, while she stood there feeling like Iris had parked that sleek red roadster directly on her chest.

"*¡Dios mío!*"

"Iris Lujan está aquí!"
"¿Te quieres casar conmigo, Iris?"

That one snagged Torien's attention. She frowned at the diminutive man, Rubén, who had blurted the spontaneous, passion-laced marriage proposal. Torien's fists clenched as possessiveness flooded her veins, choking out everything except her blazing desire to protect Iris. To claim her and challenge anyone—man or woman—to come between them. Effusiveness in the face of fame was to be expected, but when it related to Iris, Rubén's gushing bothered Torien more than she dared to admit. *Why should it, Toro? You told her no.*

The muscle in her jaw convulsed. She'd *had* to tell Iris no. It wasn't as if she'd had a choice. Hopelessness and helplessness welled up inside her, quickly fermenting to bitter resignation. Her lot in life had never bothered her before; she couldn't succumb to that useless way of thinking now.

As foreman of the worksite, however, she knew she should greet Iris. She forced her feet to move forward…one step, then another…though it took conscious and continual effort. Iris wore loose, tattered jeans, a tight white tank, and red sneakers. Her hair hung loose, face bare of makeup. Not a fancy look, but damn, Iris wore it like royalty. Her rare beauty and poise eclipsed everything around her.

Torien's gaze scraped over Iris's long, lean back as she approached her from behind. Iris was busy graciously greeting the workers, laughing and shaking hands, speaking in endearingly rudimentary Spanish. As if sensing Torien's presence like a prickle on her spine, Iris turned.

"Hi." The lone, breathy word washed over Torien in a wave of heat and longing. Intimate. The depth in those light green eyes said so much more than the single word of greeting. Iris had been cordial to the group. With Torien, there was so much more. She could feel it, could see it in Iris's vulnerable expression. She moistened her lips with a flick of her sweet, pink tongue, waiting for Torien to respond.

"Hi." Torien's heart thudded once, like the blow of a sledgehammer.

The breeze carried a strand of Iris's hair across her lips, and she brushed it away absentmindedly. "How have you been? I haven't seen you since..."

"Fine. Busy." Torien knew exactly how long it had been. Days that dragged on like lifetimes. "What are you doing here?"

As though they sensed the privacy of the exchange, the workers backed off. Torien swallowed past a tight throat, absorbing Iris with her eyes, drinking in the scent of her. She had not realized how accustomed to Iris's presence she had become. How a single intoxicating breath of Iris's sweet skin could both calm her and drive her wild. A yearning to reach for Iris overwhelmed Torien, and she stepped back to prevent her hands from giving in to the dangerous urge. She could not. Not in front of the workers, or her sister.

Or my conscience.

"I came to see where you work," Iris said lightly. Her eyes conveyed a different tone. *I'm sorry.*

I am, too, mi ángel, whispered Torien's mind. *But nothing has changed.* She swept her hand in a listless arc in front of her body. "So...here it is."

Iris crossed her arms, taking it in. She nodded with approval. "Looks like it's coming along."

"Yes." *Dear God,* Torien thought, suppressing an internal groan. This small talk could be the death of her. When Madeira approached, relief filtered through Torien like rain through loose soil. She and Iris both turned toward the younger Pacias.

Madeira smacked Torien in the shoulder with the back of her hand. "Aren't you going to introduce your favorite sister to this lovely lady, Toro?"

Torien braced herself. "Iris Lujan, my troublemaking headache of a sister, Madeira. Mosquito, this is Iris Lujan, who is a proper *lady,* so none of your usual behavior."

"You insult me," Madeira said, clearly not insulted at all.

Iris extended her hand and favored Madeira with a warm smile. "Madeira. I like that name. It's so nice to meet you. Please call me Iris."

"I would say the pleasure is all mine"—Madeira angled her head toward Toro and lowered her tone—"but we can all see the goofy look on Toro's face, so it would be a lie."

Torien frowned. *"¡Cállate!"*

Madeira laughed off Torien's stiff discomfort. "You always tell me to shut up when I hit a nerve, sister. I've told you that before. You're like an open book." She directed her attention back to Iris. "What brings you to *El Proyecto de Arco Iris?*"

Iris bent her head forward, her lush black hair tumbling over one shoulder, and fished in the pocket of her jeans. Extracting a square of newsprint, she held it up. "I read about the project needing more volunteers." A pause. "I'm here to lend a hand."

Madeira whipped an excited glance to the rest of the workers. Cupping her hands around her mouth, she announced, "Iris Lujan is going to work with us, *amigos y amigas!*"

Cheers rose, and Torien watched the dusky blush climb Iris's neck and color her cheeks, wishing she'd put that blush into her complexion in another way. But Torien couldn't take away from the moment. Bright-eyed and smiling, Iris basked in the ready acceptance of the group. Torien had never seen her looking happier or more beautiful.

But—wait. What had Iris said?

Quickly replaying it in her mind, she heard the words again. Stunned, Torien gaped. "Say that again. You are here for what?" she rasped, the words harsh after all the hearty welcomes from the others.

Iris's gaze came back to Torien, on an even level with her own. Steady, but not quite as confident as she would have liked Torien to believe. "I want to work with you, Tori. With the group." She set her jaw stubbornly as though daring Torien to deny her. "It's a worthwhile project. I'd like to donate my time."

"No. Absolutely not."

Iris's faltering bravado showed in the slight quiver of her chin. "Why not?"

"Why not? It's obvious," Torien sputtered, flailing to make sense. "Your time is more valuable, Iris. You have…you have—"

"My *time*? That's your argument? And, what—yours isn't valuable?" Iris pointed toward different people in the group, one by one. "Or her time? His? Madeira's? Isn't their time worth as much as mine?"

"That's…that's not what I meant." Torien's jaw went rigid. She would never insult the volunteers, or her sister. Blood pounded in her ears. "I am only saying—"

"It's my time, Tori, valuable or not, and I want to spend it here." She smiled, sweet and steely at once. "Okay?"

"No, not okay." Torien inched closer, her tone low. Urgent. "This isn't the kind of work for you, and you know it."

"And that's the real reason you don't want me to stay?" Her gaze, hot and wanting, dropped to Torien's lips.

God, Torien felt it like a touch…a kiss. An unexpected nibble. It swirled inside her, a raging storm.

"Or," Iris added, "is there something else beneath the surface?"

One corner of Torien's mouth lifted as the sensual hurricane moved low in her body. "Believe me, Irisíta. You don't want to know what's beneath the surface."

Iris shook her head slowly, chin lifted, expression burning with challenge. "Honey," she whispered, "that right there is where you're dead wrong."

That hurricane touched down, and white-hot desire flashed inside Torien. She scraped her bottom lip between her teeth, gratified to see the minute widening of Iris's eyes, the quickened rise and fall of her chest. Torien allowed herself another slow, deep drink of Iris's nearness, making sure to leave no doubt about her feelings, her almost debilitating desire. The hunger that could not be slaked. "You remember what I said about playing with fire, *mi ángel*, no?"

"I remember." Iris leaned in. "I guess I didn't mention that danger is my middle name."

Danger. Iris had no idea how close to the mark she'd struck. Enough! Torien must stay strong. Toying with Iris like this, teasing them both, would only lead to disaster. She didn't want to push too far and realize her breaking point. Stepping closer yet, Torien whispered, "It's a mistake, you coming here."

"I disagree." Iris crossed her arms. "You said yourself you appreciated my help in Moreno's garden. I'm not so helpless."

Confusion clouded Torien. "I have never thought you helpless. That is not the point, and you know it."

"Toro. *¡Basta!*" Madeira stepped into the conversation, looking at Torien as if she had three evil heads. "You told me yourself we needed more help. Why are you acting like this, embarrassing the lady and yourself?"

Torien ignored the zing of shame, snapping her hand out flat. "Don't interfere in a situation you know nothing about, Mosquito." She flashed her sister a warning glare. "Iris Lujan should not be cleaning up trash and broken concrete, pounding in fence rails and working in the soil. You know it as well as I."

Madeira jerked her chin in Iris's direction, her gaze challenging and serious. "She looks like a grown woman to me. Don't you think she knows her own mind? What if she wants to work with the project?"

"Yeah, what if I want to?" Bolstered by Madeira's support, Iris stood straighter, stronger still. She cocked her head to the side, same as she had that day in the *sotechado*, when she'd caught Torien half-dressed. Holding up the newspaper ad Torien had placed herself, Iris arched one eyebrow. "It says here you are short of workers. Is that true?" A tense moment yawned between them. "Tori? Is it true?" she asked again. "Yes or no."

Damnit. Iris had her in a no-win predicament *again*. If Torien refused her help, she would look ungracious in front of Iris, Madeira, and the entire team of laborers. If she accepted, she would have to survive Iris's intoxicating presence both here and at Moreno's, knowing she could not have her. Could never have her. Even knowing she wanted Iris more than anything she had ever wanted in her life.

"We'll help her if you don't want to," Madeira said, referring to herself and three others who were planting trees and setting sandstone stepping stones.

Torien blinked at her sister, distracted. Unbelievably uncomfortable.

"Did you hear me? Iris can work with us," Madeira added, in a rough, almost disgusted tone. "We'll take care of her, since you don't seem up to the task. Whatever she needs."

Torien pressed her lips in a grim line before locking eyes with this woman who was slowly but surely capturing her soul, making her doubt everything steady upon which she had based her life. She felt as if she were standing along the ocean shore, and Iris was the deceptively warm, dangerously strong undertow threatening to pull her legs out from under her. Part of Torien wanted to let go and be swept into the ocean of feelings for Iris. Another part wanted to wrench from her heady grasp and scramble for the safety of dry, solid land.

The safety of the known.

Defeated, she traced the soft curves of Iris's face with her eyes. "What are you doing, Irisíta?"

"Something worthwhile, just like you. I'm coming to work." A beat passed. *"Just like you."* She tucked her hair behind her ears and lifted her chin defiantly, her tone low enough that only Torien could hear her words. "Maybe someday this whole absurd tug-of-war will help you realize we are more alike than different. *Toro.*"

Turning heel, Iris joined Madeira and the other laborers— her new coworkers. Torien could do nothing but stand helplessly and watch her go. After a long, pain-wrought moment, she turned back to her own work. Bewildered. Frustrated. *Wanting...*

Fine.

Damnit, *fine.*

Iris could stay if she insisted.

But the slightest bit of impropriety could ruin them. Iris might not want to face that fact, but Torien must. For both of them. No matter what it took, she must resist Iris as if her very life depended on it, because, in truth, it very well might.

Struggling against Iris's fierce undertow, Torien trudged back to the safe, dry land she had grown used to...had grown into. The only bit of stability she knew.

CHAPTER SIX

H ow's it going, Iris?"
        "Great," she said, in a falsely upbeat tone. Two days
had passed since she'd joined the project, and her and Madeira's
little plan to throw her together with Torien was failing. Miserably.
Torien had hardly come near her, barely looked at her. Iris was
all too aware that her vacation was rushing to an end, and she
couldn't think of a single way to stop time.

She looked up at Madeira staring down at her, blocking the
sun, which had been dipping in and out of the gloomy clouds all
day. Much like her emotions. She had begun to accept that her
yearning for Torien was solidly one-sided, her pursuit the futile
stuff of a schoolgirl's crush. The only problem was, she didn't
think she would recover from this as quickly as she had from the
crushes of her youth.

She blinked up at Madeira again as she loomed above her,
arms crossed, biceps bulging, a sympathetic smile on her face.
Embarrassment suffused Iris for having dragged Madeira into this
hot mess. "We're getting a lot done," Iris said brightly, referring
to the project.

Madeira lowered to the ground and sat cross-legged in front
of her, elbows on her knees and fingers steepled against her lips.
After a moment, Madeira said, "I meant, how are things going
with my bullheaded sister?"

"Oh. That." Humiliation swept Iris's gaze to the ground. She shrugged, trying to keep the brittle, shaky smile pasted on her face. "Okay, I guess. I'm still here." She tried to chuckle, but it came out sounding more like a nerve-shot sob. *Damn.* Madeira was far too attuned to others' emotions to have missed it, and Iris cringed inwardly.

"Has she spoken to you?"

Iris hedged. "Some." A moment passed, and her tone came out sounding less enthusiastic. "Actually…not really."

"¡Maldita sea!" Madeira ground her teeth, her fists clenching vigorously. "I swear, I could kill her."

"No, please. Don't be angry." Iris reached out and squeezed Madeira's tight knuckles, then folded her hands listlessly in her lap. "We made a mistake trying to force things, Madi. Your sister isn't interested."

"No. She is. I can see it. I know it."

The burn of unshed tears assaulted Iris's nose, but she struggled for a breezy tone, unwilling to allow Madeira to blame herself for this debacle. "Let's just forget it, okay? I'm enjoying working on the project, and that's really the point."

"It's not the point."

"Well, it has *become* the point. Besides…" Iris trailed off, cold claws of anxiety stabbing her chest. She slanted Madeira a worried glance, but couldn't bear to continue. She had hoped the little fantasy about her and Torien hooking up—falling in love, even—would work out, that she wouldn't have to tell Madeira she was only in Denver temporarily. Now she knew the whole thing had been just that—a fantasy—and she had to come clean, like it or not.

Her hands trembled. Would Madeira think Iris had deceived her? That she was a pure, selfish idiot for trying to get close to Torien when Jolie Cosmetique virtually owned her life? Would Madi imagine Iris had only been out for a quick, meaningless fling with Torien, the woman for whom she obviously cared so deeply?

No. Couldn't happen. Iris simply must convince Madi that wasn't true.

Just spit it out. With a deep, stabilizing breath, she launched. "Madeira, I should have told you this before, but, um…"

"What?"

"I…I have an assignment," she whispered, moisture pooling in her eyes. "For work."

Maderia's expression brightened. "That's wonderful!"

"No." She waved off the praise. "Not so much. Let me finish." A pause ensued. "It's a three-year gig, and"—she swallowed—"it's in…France."

Madeira's face slackened with dismay. "Oh, no."

"I know. Between you and me, I'm not looking forward to it. Don't get me wrong—it's a dream job. One I would've killed for ten years ago." She bit her lip and begged forgiveness with her eyes. "I'm sorry I didn't tell you. I thought…oh, I don't know what I thought. Doesn't matter, though. I should have told you from the very beginning."

After a moment, Madeira's mouth closed, and she swallowed convulsively. "When must you go?"

"Three weeks," Iris said, barely audible. "A little less, actually. I signed the contract months ago, before Tori and I even met, but I'd been wrestling with it for a long time. Wrestling with my life. Then I met your sister and you"—she smiled—"all of you, and I stopped thinking about it for a bit. I wanted to…forget. But it's there. Like a vulture, picking over the bones of my world. And…I have to go." Iris traced small heart shapes in the soil with one finger. "Which I guess won't matter anyway."

Silence hung between them for several moments.

"Iris, can I ask you something?"

She nodded.

Madeira's eyes searched her face. "If things were different with Torien…would you still go?"

Iris's heart began pounding toward an unexpected crescendo, harder and louder until she could scarcely hear her own thoughts.

She had been truthful with Madeira about her feelings from the beginning. Why stop now?

Shaking her head, she said, "I would have found a way to stay. Ridiculous, I know. I'm getting way ahead of myself, of this whole…crazy thing." She watched Madi for long, pained moments. "I…I guess I was grasping."

"What do you mean?"

Iris flipped her hand, a weak, ineffectual motion, which was exactly how she felt. "It's not all about Torien. My family is here, too, and leaving them has always been hard." *But Torien would have been the perfect excuse to break that contract and stay.* "The thing is, something's been missing in my life for a long time, and I never could pinpoint what it was. Until I met your sister." Iris scrunched her nose. "Does that sound stupid?"

"Not at all."

As relief drained through her like cool peppermint, Iris twisted her mouth to the side. "That mysterious missing thing? Now I know what it was, thanks to Tori. But"—she sighed—"it doesn't look like that's going to pan out."

Madeira scrubbed her hands over her face, pushing a rough breath through her fingers.

"Look, it doesn't matter," Iris tried to assure her, wondering if she should have tempered her honesty a bit. "I appreciate your help more than you know. But I shouldn't look to Tori as my proverbial knight in shining armor. If I want to change my life, *I* have to do it."

"True, but if Toro knew—"

"No," Iris said in a rush. "Torien has enough responsibility as it is without worrying how her decisions will affect me. I'm a grown woman. You said it yourself. If she knew about my dilemma, she'd probably pretend to be interested in me, just to make my choice easier. Tori has to want me for *me* or not at all." Iris smiled sadly, then squeezed Maderia's arm with affection that was easy to give. "Please don't tell her."

"I won't. Don't worry."

"Promise me." Iris bit her lip until it stung.

Madeira nodded. "If you make me one promise, too."

"Anything," Iris said.

Madeira clasped Iris's hand between both of hers, eyes beseeching. "Don't give up on Toro. Not yet."

❖

"She is doing a good job, Toro."

The words at the back of her neck brought Torien's head around.

Madeira gave a small nod in Iris's direction then added almost belligerently, "Don't you agree?"

Torien had been so caught up in staring at Iris engaged in easy camaraderie with Rubén and Natán, she had not heard her sister approach. "Mmm," she grunted, refocusing on her work. She hadn't been in a talkative mood for days. A trickle of sweat traveled the length of her spine, despite the massive thunderheads that striped the worksite with shadows.

"Is that a yes?" Madeira demanded.

"Yes, Mosquito, it is," she said in exasperation, wondering why Madeira was so damn angry.

"Have you told her she's doing a good job?"

The motion of Torien's hands stilled while she forced her words into a patient tone. "No, I have not told her. I've been a little busy, if you haven't noticed." For two days, Iris had worked with them. For two excruciating days, Torien had ached for her company yet denied herself the pleasure of it simply to keep the world spinning as it should. If anyone had a right to feel testy, it was she.

Though Iris worked no more than fifty feet away, it felt like a continent separated them, and jealousy spiked every time she thought of her laughing and working alongside the other volunteers. But she had planted herself into this position, and the roots ran deep. If she had welcomed Iris like they had, Iris might be working next to *her*, like she had at Moreno's what seemed…a lifetime ago.

If life were different.

If she were free.

If, if, if.

God, she yearned for that closeness again.

Torien shook off the what-ifs and peered at her sister. "You were talking to her earlier, no?"

"I was," Madeira said.

"Did *you* praise her?"

Madeira frowned. "Of course I did, but she should hear it from you. She *needs* to hear it from you. You're the foreman."

For a moment Torien let the sounds of the life around them and the smell of the soil consume her, then her eyes lifted toward Iris again of their own volition. "Are the workers getting too familiar with her?" she asked, with feigned nonchalance she knew her sister wouldn't buy, not for a split second.

"What do you care?"

"Don't be stupid," Torien snapped.

A long sigh emptied Madeira's lungs. "She's happy working here, Toro. She likes them. They like her."

"That's what I am afraid of," Torien murmured gravely. "I don't want anyone to treat her badly. Take advantage."

"Since when did our *socios* become a pack of animals in your eyes?" Madeira asked. "Or are you just marking territory in your mind? Ridiculous, since you refuse to claim it in the real world anyway."

Torien closed her eyes and exhaled through clenched teeth. She and Madeira had been snapping at each other like wild dogs ever since Iris had begun working with them. Torien hadn't yet figured out why, but now was not the time to explore it, whether Madeira goaded her or not. "I don't know what your problem is, but I'm not in the mood for this."

Madeira swore and shook her head. "Of course you aren't. But let me ease your back-breaking worry, *hermana*. Iris is fine."

Sarcasm laced her words. She lowered to her knees and set about helping with the sweet william they had procured at the nursery earlier that day, both of their movements jerky and impatient. "Not only that, but Iris is not your responsibility. She can take care of herself."

"My baby sister"—Torien snorted—"the goddamned expert of everything."

Madeira grabbed her arm, eyes serious. "That's not it, Toro. Damn! You treat her like she might break into a million pieces. She isn't made of glass, you know. She is flesh and blood and all woman. Can't you see how much she wishes you realized that?"

Torien's stomach tightened; she shrugged off Madeira's grip. If anyone knew Iris was pure flesh and blood, it was she. And, she didn't need schooling from her cocksure little sister. "I do realize it. I am only trying to protect her." *From myself. From this.*

"Wake up!" Madeira pierced the soil bed with a vehement stab of the trowel. "She doesn't want or need your protection. She wants you to care about her, woman to woman. She wants *you*. How can you be so blind?" Madeira smacked away a trickle of sweat with the back of her hand. "I am seven years younger, Toro, and I have to spell this out? It's pathetic."

Madeira rarely gave in to anger, and the outburst snagged Torien's attention. An answering frustration flared from a hidden place deep within her, but she fought to control it, to keep her tone steady. "I am not blind, Madeira. Don't imagine you see things I do not. But your life and mine are different." Indeed, Torien didn't mark time with a series of red-lit trysts in various women's beds, like her footloose little sister did. Torien had responsibilities, obligations, worries. "What would you have me do, since you know everything?" she rasped. "Turn my back on all of it for her?"

"Iris doesn't want that!"

"As if you know." Torien flicked her hand in disgust.

"Do *you* know? Have you even asked her?"

"I cannot concentrate on what she wants, Madeira. She is

the guest of *Señora* Moreno. My employer. She is *Iris Lujan*, for God's sake. Use your damn brain." Torien scrambled to her feet and stalked to a trash bin, discarding an empty flat that had held the fledgling plants with a rough thrust.

"She *is* Iris Lujan, *sí*." Madeira followed, unwilling to let the subject go. "And you are Torien Pacias. That squeaky guy in Disneyland with the big ears? He's Mickey Mouse. So what? None of that matters. Follow your heart instead of your brain for once."

Madeira snaked a hand around Torien's arm again—the last straw. Torien twisted violently from her grasp, whirling to wad a fistful of Madeira's shirt in her palm. She pulled her sister's face close and lowered her tone so the others wouldn't hear them. "And just what do you suggest, Mosquito, eh?" Torien asked. "That I handle her like you would? Lose myself in some romantic fantasy? Kiss her? Make love to her?"

"Of course not," Madeira scoffed. "Not *Toro*, who is immune to the needs and desires of mortal women."

"And then toss her aside? Lose my job?" Torien spat, unheeded, her yearning for Iris fueling her anger, making Madeira the target of her bitter words. "Lose this house? Leave *Mamá* in the lurch next month because a woman grabbed hold of my heart? Don't be a fucking fool—"

"*¡Basta, hermana!*" This time Madeira wrenched away, then advanced on Torien again. Fists locked and loaded at her sides, eyes flashing. Fury quickened their breathing. "Enough of the family, your job, your reputation, your damned tiresome burden. If you are afraid or you have no interest in Iris, fine. Be a woman and admit it. But don't use *us* as your excuse anymore." Madeira pounded a fist on her chest. "I am a woman, too. Don't discount my place in the family or what I contribute."

Startled, Torien blinked. "I...I don't discount you, Mo—"

"No?" Madeira huffed, her short laugh humorless. "You are not responsible for me. For the whole world."

They stared, chests heaving, arms stiff and angry.

Madeira's outburst and its resulting guilt left Torien mute and stunned. Did she truly make her sister feel useless? Did she hide behind the responsibilities of her family? Contrition tightened her throat and rushed in her ears like a train. She opened her mouth to respond, then closed it, hung her head, and ran the fingers of both hands slowly through her hair, interlocking them behind her neck. "Damnit."

Life was spiraling out of her control. She felt as if she were sliding down the steep side of a mountain flailing for a finger hold or clump of grass—anything to slow her descent, all because she was falling for a woman. She wanted to let go and fall—God, how she wanted to. But just as her far too insightful sister had accused, she was afraid.

Afraid to fail.

Afraid not to.

Afraid to disappoint those who depended on her.

Too late. Clearly, she had already disappointed Madeira, though for a very different reason than she had imagined. "I never meant to belittle your contributions."

Madeira's palm closed on her shoulder and did not move away. "*De nada.* What do *you* want, Toro?" she asked softly.

Lips pursed, forehead wrinkled in consternation, Torien peered at her little sister, her sidekick. The person who claimed to know her better than she knew herself.

"What would you want?" Madeira implored. "If there were no job worries, no bills, no burden on your soul? What would be your big dream now?"

Torien and her big dreams. She snorted sardonically, but the sound was weak. She had given up on those big dreams when *Papá* died. Didn't Madeira realize they weren't carefree children anymore? The interminable nothingness stretched between them as their gazes locked. Sister to sister, silent communication so much clearer than muddled words.

"Tell me."

I would want her, whispered Torien's mind. She shook her head against the thought.

"Say it," Madeira urged.

Say it, Toro. What could it hurt to verbalize the wish? "A chance with Iris," was all she managed to say.

"There. Was that so hard?"

"Yes. Because I can't have it."

Acknowledgment settled dully in Madeira's eyes along with a sad, pleading look. "Damnit, Toro, yes you can. Reach for your dream before you lose your chance. No one ever asked you to sacrifice your whole life for *la familia*. You've done enough."

The uncertainty she felt must have showed, because her sister added, "All those times we called you the dreamer? That wasn't an insult." Madeira let that sink in. "Did you think it was?"

Torien never broke the stare with Madeira.

"We looked up to you, Toro. We still do. You had us then, you will have us always, no matter what. We're your family. We love you."

"But *Papá*—"

"Forget *Papá*. You aren't *Papá*. When he died, you gave us hope for something…greater with your big, exciting dreams. Especially me." Madeira shook her head. "Don't make me realize it was all empty talk, Toro. All that stuff about making our deepest wishes come true. Don't give up on that now, when you finally have a chance for something amazing. For the chance to realize one of your big dreams."

Torien watched her sister walk away, shoulders slumped with defeat. For a long time, she stood dumbfounded. Stunned.

She hadn't understood the animosity crackling between her and Madeira before.

Now she knew. Madeira just wanted her to wake up. To see the light.

To live.

Damnit, the little mosquito was right, much as Torien hated

to say it. But Torien was the oldest, and when *Papá* died, she didn't think twice before taking over the role he'd never really fulfilled. But that decision had come from a place of bitterness, of resignation. Of disgust. *Papá* had died in that factory accident. Not Torien. Instead of slipping into their father's role—working herself to death in jobs for which she held no passion, all for the sake of the family—Madeira simply wanted her big sister to define her own role. To enjoy life.

I will try, Mosquito. I will.

Torien released a short groan of laughter at the irony of it all, then glanced around the worksite for Iris. After a moment of confusion, she realized Iris was gone. Her gaze strayed to the street just as the little red Mercedes zipped around the corner and disappeared.

Finally awake, and still she had missed her chance.

Typical.

Humbled, Torien shook her head. She guessed she did have lessons to learn from her flashy *hermanita* after all.

Feeling stronger for having accepted the reality of their situation, Iris made her way down to Geraline's gardens that evening, intent on apologizing to Torien. She hadn't heard a word of the argument between Madeira and her at the worksite today, but everyone could see from their rigid stances and angry eyes that it had been vehement. And all Iris's fault, she felt certain, which had shocked her into a painful realization. She had brought nothing but problems and pain into Torien's peaceful world with her selfishness, and it had to stop.

She had left Círculo de Esperanza immediately, telling Rubén and Natán she had an appointment she had forgotten. Really, she needed to get away and pull her head together. After a long talk with Paloma and an intimate date with a Godiva chocolate bar (okay, two), she felt more settled. Resolute. She refused to come between sisters who were obviously so close, and she had no right to foist herself on Torien if the woman just plain didn't want her. That had been her most egregious mistake, one for which she would make amends.

A cool, ominous wind lifted her hair, swirling it around her shoulders, left bare by her silk tank top. She was glad she'd chosen a pair of fitted jeans to go with it. The moon hid behind a thick layer of clouds, and she could tell from the way the cottonwood leaves had flipped that a rainstorm brewed. Still, the sweetness in the air reminded her poignantly of the night she'd first met Torien. The way Tori had soothed her with a calm gentleness, the deep love in her words when she spoke of her family.

Iris's throat closed with desire she couldn't act upon but wouldn't deny, either. It hadn't been so long ago that they'd met, but it felt like a lifetime. Three lifetimes. She had learned a lot from Torien over the weeks, lessons about life and choices, about risk and responsibility and missed opportunities. From here on out, she would make a conscious effort to change her life, though she hadn't decided how she would execute that scary first step. But she had a goal. That was a start. She wasn't sitting on the sidelines watching a practice match of her life anymore. Whatever it took, she would leap directly into the fray.

She paused at the gazebo, so ready to see Torien she could hardly breathe, but—Iris glanced around—Tori wasn't there. She strained her eyes to search the quickly darkening gardens, goose bumps washing over her bare arms. Shivering, she rubbed the chilled skin with her palms. *Callused* palms, she noted with a smile. Baby calluses, still sore to the touch, but they were there nonetheless, and they were *hers*. She had earned them, and damn, that felt better than she'd ever imagined it would.

She strolled to the little grassy oasis hidden behind the lilac bushes where Torien had told her their lives didn't mesh; no sign of her there, either. Torien probably hadn't come to Geraline's tonight, Iris admitted with a pang of sorrow, and how could she blame her? If she had met someone who brought nothing but trouble and turmoil and temptation to her otherwise peaceful life, she would steer clear, too.

Seized with disappointment, Iris turned back toward the house, but the melodic sounds of softly strummed guitar strings caught her attention. The eerie sound floated toward her from the *cabaña*, Torien's erstwhile residence. Hope straightened Iris's shoulders and fluttered beneath her breastbone.

Tori was here. Not working, but…here.

Palms suddenly moist, Iris took a breath for courage and headed in that direction. She peered around the corner of the small house and saw Torien before Torien caught sight of her. Tori sat in a cane-backed chair, tipped so its front legs angled off the ground. Her broad, strong back rested against the house, and the guitar sat nestled in her lap, her fingers slowly finessing the strings, those deep, dark eyes at half mast. An open wine bottle sat on the floor next to the chair, along with a nearly empty glass.

Torien looked as if she had just showered, pulled clothes over her still-damp body. Iris's yearning to touch her lips to Torien's jawline nearly overpowered her, but she gripped a tree trunk, staving off the need. Intending to greet Torien as casually as possible, Iris opened her mouth, but the words would not come.

Right on cue, Iris froze. And snapped a branch off the tree.

All at once, Torien became aware she wasn't alone. Her eyes flew open and met Iris's. The legs of the chair hit the cement patio floor with a clunk; down went the guitar. Just like that, Torien stood in front of her. Eye to eye, mouth to mouth, heartbeat to heartbeat, as Iris had always known it would be. As if they were made to fit together.

How to start such a conversation, she wondered? Waiting wouldn't make it any easier. She might as well jump into that fray…starting now. She cleared her throat, then said, her voice thin and papery, "You aren't working."

Torien shrugged, studying her. "I work too much, or so my hotheaded baby sister thinks." One side of her mouth lifted.

"Madi's smart, and she's right."

"Madi, huh? Maybe so," Torien conceded.

Okay. Buck up. She could do this. "Is everything…okay?" She tucked her hair behind her ears, then crossed her arms beneath her breasts. "With Madeira, I mean?"

Torien's eyes warmed with wry affection, seeing a picture somewhere inside. "We are hot-blooded Latina sisters. We argue. The anger never lasts." Thunder rumbled fluorescent red in a black thunderhead hanging over the mountains. "A storm is on the way."

"I noticed."

"Can you smell the rain, Irisíta?"

She nodded. "It smells good."

"Like new beginnings, no?"

She studied Torien's face, trying not to read into her words, fighting not to allow her gaze to drop to—God—to those lips. "The…um…moisture will be good for the plants."

"As long as it isn't a downpour," Torien said, worried eyes tracking the far-off storm on the horizon. "Flowers are delicate when newly planted. Like ideas. Or dreams. They must be nourished gently. Slowly. Not drowned all at once."

Torien had a poetic streak, but was she trying to tell Iris something this time? Did she dare hope Tori'd had a change of heart?

"Where did you go today?" Torien turned back. "I looked for you but you were gone."

Iris sighed. "I…had to go. I should've told you, but…" Okay, so she wasn't quite as ready as she'd thought. She couldn't continue down this path of conversation, because she knew it eventually led to good-bye. *Not ready yet.* "I didn't know you played the guitar."

Torien shot a glance at the instrument, then leaned one shoulder against the front of the house. "I don't play it well, but I enjoy it. Long ago, I dreamed of being a musician."

"What happened?"

Torien pressed her lips together, the corners turning down in a thoughtful angle. "Life," she said simply.

"I'm sorry," Iris blurted, not referring to the music.

"For what?"

"For…causing problems. At the worksite. For the argument."

"It isn't you, *mi ángel*. You are doing a wonderful job there. Everyone loves you." Torien ducked her chin, eyes smiling beneath the serious gaze. "Have I told you that?"

Iris realized she ached for Torien's approval, soaking up her words like a thirsty plant. Her insides felt tender, so close to tears. She was falling in love with a woman she couldn't have. A woman who didn't want her love. How foolish was that? She shook her head. "No, you haven't told me."

"Then I have been an idiot, and it is my turn to apologize." Torien reached up to stroke Iris's cheekbone with the back of her hand. Down the slope of her cheek to her jawline, across to her chin. Her thumb smoothed over Iris's bottom lip briefly, tugging her mouth slightly open and rattling Iris's composure completely, before Torien turned her hand over and cupped the side of Iris's face.

Iris melted into the caress, closing her eyes. So much for her resolve. How could she possibly turn Torien loose when she was the one who'd become so ensnared? Unable to stop herself, Iris reached up and grabbed Torien's hand, pressing her palm against her upper chest, holding it there, wanting to pull Tori inside her heart forever. Locked. No key. The pad of Torien's index finger dipped into the hollow at Iris's throat, an utterly sensual touch, and Iris allowed her eyes to flutter closed for a blip of a moment.

"I am a stubborn woman, Irisíta."

"And I am a pushy woman."

They shared an apologetic smile.

"Can we start over?"

"Always. But what does that mean, start over? Nothing has changed, Tori. We still come from different worlds." Iris blinked back stinging tears, just as the storm cloud mirrored her emotions and began to patter the earth with raindrops.

"I know that more than anyone. But we can be friends, no? Weren't we always friends?" The rain came harder, seeming to enclose them in a curtain of safety.

"Yes." If that was all she could have of Torien, she would take it. She brushed rivulets rainwater from her face, then Torien's. "You still want that?"

"More than anything."

Shaky with relief, she released Torien's hand and banged the back of her fist playfully against Torien's soaked shoulder. A wobbly half-laugh, half-sob escaped before Iris could control it. "Damnit, Tori, you make me crazy. I came here to tell you good-bye, you know. To quit the project."

Torien laughed softly and pulled her into a gentle embrace, tucking Iris's forehead into the crook of her strong neck. Around them, the storm intensified, battering the lilac bushes, releasing their sweet scent into the air. "You cannot. The men work harder when you are there, probably hoping to impress you. And so do most of the women."

"As if." Iris only wanted to impress Torien. Didn't she know that by now? Chilled, half drenched, Iris shivered and nestled closer. "I don't want to keep at it if it bothers you." Thunder rolled above them, followed by a single, iridescent bolt of lightning.

"Everything about you bothers me, *querida*, but that's not always a bad thing, and I don't want you to go." Torien lifted Iris's head, cupping her cheeks with softly curved palms. Her lips slowly raised into a smile that glittered in the depths of her eyes. "Okay?"

Iris bit the corner of her mouth to keep it from trembling. "Okay," she whispered. "Tori?"

"Yes?"

"It's really pouring out here. And my tank top is silk."

They laughed. "Come." Torien took her hand. "Drink wine with me, *mi ángel*, until the rain passes. And then we must both sleep. Our day will start early."

"Yes, it will."

"And beginning tomorrow, Irisíta…you work with me."

CHAPTER SEVEN

Initially, Iris had yearned to prove to Torien and the others she wasn't some pampered, high-maintenance woman, which was how she and Madeira had come up with their ill-hatched plan in the first place. But the longer she worked with *El Proyecto de Arco Iris*, the more it became about the project and the less about proving a rather pointless…point. She loved the mission of the group, believed in it. Gardening was satisfying in itself, but creating an oasis of beauty in a place where she knew people would really appreciate it—yeah, that was indescribable. She knew, as she dug in the earth, that *this* was the feeling she'd been missing in her life. The sense that what she did with her days truly mattered.

After the initial excitement of her arrival, no one seemed to question her presence, even those who weren't working on the project. The volunteers were grateful for every helping hand, of course, and the area residents were more curious and excited about the flowers, trees, and benches than the volunteers planting them.

She glanced around as afternoon sunshine gilded the houses surrounding the square. Little sun-browned children played in the yards and cul-de-sacs, their voices rife with excitement and joy, while whichever parent or adult was present watched them. Truly, the village raised the children here. Dressed-to-impress teenagers joked and bumped shoulders as they walked around the square, iPods firmly in place.

Women sat on front porches together, head-and-tailing their green beans or cleaning pintos. Old, proper men, wearing slacks, freshly pressed *guayaberas*, and fedoras, claimed porch benches and lawn chairs facing the garden. Their skinny legs crossed, gnarled hands resting atop their canes, they tracked the volunteers' progress with expressions that sent the clear message that they were accustomed to being in charge.

Real life. Burgeoning, pulsating, breathing real life.

The neighborhood might not be a wealthy one, but it overflowed with pride, brimming with the quick laughter and simple passions of people who didn't need much to be happy. The new garden would only help the community grow closer. If it was up to Iris, she would bring community gardens into less fortunate neighborhoods everywhere, work in the soil alongside Torien and the others. Ah, heaven. The stuff of dreams.

Dreams for people who haven't signed three-year modeling contracts overseas.

With a pang of envy for the regular volunteers, Iris wished she belonged to this landscape instead of just visiting it. She felt more at home there than she had anywhere else in a long time, yet she was an outsider and always would be.

The ironic thing was, if she told most Denver suburbanites she yearned to be a part of the Círculo de Esperanza community, incredulity would abound. A *poor* neighborhood. A *bad* neighborhood. A *dangerous* neighborhood. *El barrio.* God…they had no idea how wrong they were.

Torien had kept her moonlit promises of starting anew, a fact that pleased Iris no end. They had worked together for two days filled with easy smiles, casual conversation, and spontaneous teasing. Gradually, Iris settled into this acceptance, into the sense that Torien appreciated her presence just as much as the others did.

A long, cool shadow fell across the soil bed where she'd been busily planting purple coneflowers for the last several hours. She looked up and cocked a brow playfully. *Speak of the sexy devil.* "You make a better door than a window."

Confusion undulated over Torien's expression. "I don't understand."

"It's a colloquialism, like one of yours. A saying. In this case, it means you're blocking my sun."

"Ah." Torien stepped to the side, then smiled. "Doing okay?"

Iris indicated the half-moon pattern she had finished, proud of her work but striving for nonchalance. "You're the foreman— you tell me." She felt starved for Torien's approval, though Tori handed it out freely to everyone on the project. Still, Iris couldn't get enough. Torien might be stoic and super Type-A when it came to her responsibilities, but she had a kind, appreciative way with people that rang of sincerity and inspired everyone to work even harder.

Torien soaked it in and nodded slowly, as though deep in thought. "Looks good. There is only one problem."

Startled, Iris retraced the path of Torien's scrutiny. She thought she'd followed her directions to the letter. "Oh no. What?"

"The planting looks perfect, don't worry. But…" Squatting before Iris, Torien quirked her mouth and lifted the tail of her own shirt to wipe Iris's chin. "You manage to get covered in dirt every day, and I just can't figure out how you do it." Her voice softened to a purr that resonated against Iris's chest and hardened her nipples. "It's a soil bed, *mi ángel*, not a swimming pool."

"Very funny," Iris said, with feigned haughtiness. She pulled back, smearing her face with the crook of her elbow. An image of the Peanuts character Pig-Pen flashed in her mind. "I'm no dirtier than the rest of you."

"Irisíta," Torien said patiently. "You are dirtier than the dirt itself. Pretty soon you will sprout."

Iris laughed. "I just have a passion for my work."

"Yes, you do. And it shows beautifully all over you." Torien reached out and smeared mud off the tip of Iris's nose with the pad of her thumb, examining it and then turning it toward her as if to prove her point. "What would those magazine photographers think if they could see you now?"

Iris grimaced, not wanting the ugly reminders of Real Life—which felt less real by the minute—to mar this picture-perfect day. Real Life, however, was flapping its vulture wings and swooping down to gobble up her happiness. Soon. She deftly coned up another plug of soil, then blinked at Torien through her lashes. "Would it embarrass you to be seen in public with me looking like this?"

"Depends. Would I take you dancing looking like a mud ball?" Torien shrugged. "Probably not."

Iris knew she was teasing, but the thought of Torien taking her dancing fluttered her stomach. "Actually, it was an honest question." She held out her forearms for inspection and, realizing they really did look super trashed, she brushed them off, without much success. The loamy soil just smeared, from her palms to her arms and back.

Torien cocked her head questioningly. "¿Qué? Is something on your mind?"

"Nothing major. Errands, to-do lists. You know how it is."

"I do. Anything I can do to help?"

"Actually…my car is due for service. I'm supposed to leave it at the garage down on Broadway this afternoon." Iris bestowed her best winning smile. "What would it take to get you to follow me, then drive me back to Geraline's? They'll drop off the car when it's done."

"What would it take? Hmm." Torien crossed her arms, sunlight shining through the sparse hair that dusted them to the smooth, bronze skin underneath. "Here is a free tip. Never ask a red-blooded Latina that question."

"I'm a red-blooded Latina."

"Hmm." Torien conceded the point.

"Plus, you are a red-blooded Latina with honor, right? So you don't count."

"Well, *hijole*, since I don't count—"

"Tori…you know what I meant."

Torien flashed a quick grin. "It isn't a problem. When must we leave?"

Iris warmed from the inside out. God, it felt good to know she had finally broken through some of Tori's carefully erected walls of propriety and duty. A week ago, Torien would never have shared a car with her. How would that look? What would people think? Pros. Cons. Risks.

Iris figured she'd go for the gold since Tori had been so amenable to the first suggestion. "Whenever. How about if I repay you with dinner?"

"Not necessary."

"Since when does necessity have anything to do with a dinner invitation?" Iris's desire for Tori to accept morphed into raw determination. "Let me do it anyway. Please?"

That old bedfellow, *doubt*, drifted over Torien's expression. "I have much work to do…I don't know."

"At the estate? I can help."

"Iris," Torien said in a gently warning tone.

Her arms spread in an open shrug. "What? You said I could help when you were there."

Torien gave that one to Iris, inclining her head. "I still don't have time to go out to dinner."

"No problem." Iris began to plan the menu in her head. "You have a kitchen in the *cabaña*, don't you? I'll cook."

"You cook?" Skepticism played like a tattoo on Torien's face.

"Hey, don't look so doubtful." She glared, albeit playfully. "I come from a long line of women who cooked three meals a day, every day."

"And I come from a long line of *vaqueros*, but you don't see me on the back of a horse." Torien's delectable lips quivered with amusement. "When was the last time you cooked?"

"You know, it isn't every day I offer to cook for a woman, *Toro*." Reaching out, Iris smacked Torien's sculpted shoulder with the heel of her hand, leaving a dirty smudge. "You should feel honored."

Torien laughed lightly. "Tell me one thing."

"What?"

"Are you going to wash your hands first?"

The clump of dirt she scooped and threw hit Torien square in the side of the neck. "You're so funny. Not. Let me *prove* to you I can cook," she said, with an arched eyebrow of challenge. "I'll even bet you something."

"What?"

"I don't know. I'll think about it. If you like my food, I win. If not, it's all you."

Torien stared at her for several moments, then nodded once. "Okay, it is a deal. My kitchen is open to you. I will even clean up," she added, magnanimously.

"Whoo-boy, you're an easy mark."

"What does that mean?" Torien stood, then offered a palm and pulled Iris to her feet.

Iris brushed off the seat of her shorts with both hands. "It means, if I had known you were a gambling woman, I would have wagered a hell of a lot more than dinner." She turned and flounced toward a water hose, feeling Tori's gaze burning into her back the whole way. God, that felt good. *Score one for Iris.*

❖

Squeaky clean, and dressed in her most comfortable, ankle-length red sundress, Iris bent to open the stove and pour topping over the buttermilk baked chicken. It was her favorite recipe, passed on by her friend Cyn—a prominent runway model with decidedly down-home Texas roots. She had considered preparing a specialty Mexican dish to remind Torien of home, but the truth was, it *had* been a long time since she'd cooked. Buttermilk baked chicken was nearly impossible to screw up, and even when you did, it still tasted great.

She'd told Torien what she—Iris—would win in the bet if Tori liked her dinner, and she wore a vivid reminder of what was at stake. Big, red letters spelled KISS THE COOK across the chest of her black apron. As she basted, Iris smirked. Torien's discomfort with the situation was worth the whole evening.

After scrubbing her hands, Iris turned to Torien, who wore crisp jeans and fitted black T-shirt. Iris hadn't realized how breath-stealing-hot such simple garments could look on a woman who needed no embellishments. Oblivious to Iris's blatant admiration, Tori pawed through a drawer for a corkscrew. Locating one, she wound it into the top of the wine bottle with strong twists that flexed her triceps and the finely honed muscles in her upper back.

A question had been on Iris's mind since that afternoon, and staring at Tori's physique brought it to the fore. "Do you really come from a long line of *vaqueros*?" She'd fallen in love with many a fictional cowgirl, with their sensually rugged faces and rough hands. The Mexican cowgirls were the sexiest of the sexy, and she had no doubt Torien could have a bit of that blood in her veins.

Torien glanced over her shoulder at Iris, one side of her mouth lifted in amusement. "I am *Mexicana*. We all descend from the *vaqueros*."

"Ah, so it's one of those kinds of tales." Iris accepted the glass of wine Torien had poured, then said, "Tell me the real story. I've heard about your mom and the twins. What was your father like?"

Tori's focus drifted to that faraway place for a second.

Shaking it off, she pointed toward the door. "Shall we sit outside? I noticed the honeysuckle in full bloom earlier. The air will smell like magic."

Iris nodded, and when they'd settled onto the porch, the chicken timer ticking on the small table between them, Iris looked at her expectantly.

Torien said, "*Papá* was a dreamer," in a disapproving tone. She might as well have said, "*Papá* was a murderer."

Odd. Iris had always admired people who aimed high and set goals. Was this not the case in Torien's world? She watched the hummingbirds visit the honeysuckle, caught sight of a few small bats swooping down to rid the air of mosquitoes. Somewhere in the hedge, crickets had begun to chirp. Gorgeous evening. Gorgeous company. Tough conversation. "But that's a good thing, right? To dream?"

Torien's lips curled down at the edges, and she shrugged. "Not always. To *Papá*, the grand adventure was always just over the hill, around the next bend, hanging on the red gleam of the horizon at sunset. He never seemed happy with what he had for too long." Tori flashed a look of shame. "I do not mean to speak badly of my father. I loved him. Still do."

"No, I understand." Iris suddenly remembered Madeira saying the family called Torien "the dreamer," and the parallel intrigued her. Tori had probably always been compared to her father. *The father who had disappointed her.* That would certainly explain a lot. "It's clear that you love him. Look how you've taken care of the family in his absence."

A sad smile played at the corners of Torien's lips. She deftly brushed aside Iris's comment by simply ignoring it. "*Papá* would find a job and work hard for a while, but the better job, the more exciting offer, the get-rich-quick scheme would draw him, like…" She lifted her chin toward the golden spill of honeysuckle over the wrought iron fence. "Like the flowers draw the bees. Over and over." She scoffed quietly. "Never mind the wife and four children at home."

"But he was a good man, right?" Iris asked, softly. "Didn't he die in a work accident?"

"*Sí.*" A muscle in Torien's jaw worked briefly as torment gleamed in her moist eyes. One foot began to bounce, as if Torien's body was trying to release pent-up steam. "A factory he had only worked in for a short time. He didn't like it there. I guess I can't blame him for that. It was a"—she gestured an arc from one hand to a distant spot in the air—"*puente*...you understand? A bridge from one job to the next better one."

"What happened?"

"*Papá* did not take the proper time to learn the safety procedures for the factory, since he did not plan to stay long." Her expression deepened with pain, the scant lines bracketing her mouth tightening. "It was his fault," Torien said, in little more than a whisper.

Iris blinked, confused. "What was?"

"The explosion." Torien's voice broke, and she paused, pressing her lips together. "Ten hardworking people died. And it was my father's fault."

Iris's abdomen contracted with shock and horror. She reached across the little table and laid her hand on Torien's knee. "God, I'm so sorry."

Torien covered Iris's hand and squeezed. For a long moment, she didn't speak. After a sip of wine and a deep swallow, she said, "I realize it was an accident. But I was...I was so very angry for a long time, Iris. *Papá* and his big dreams, and we were all made to suffer." A sigh. "I'm not proud of those emotions. But...I felt them."

Wow. How to comfort a woman whose entire life had changed due to one careless action of a parent? The action of a man who was supposed to take care of Torien? Of the whole family? "Where were you when it happened?"

"Home. Getting ready to go..." Torien clamped back the statement, raked fingers angrily through her hair.

"Where, Tori?"

Torien clicked her tongue as if the topic epitomized idiocy and selfishness, all the things she was not. She met Iris's gaze, a rueful, grim half-smile on her face. "To college. That was *my* big dream, and I had finally earned an opportunity. A scholarship. Then *Papá* died, and I was needed at home."

"Oh...honey, that's awful. Did you lose it? The scholarship?"

A beat passed. "Yes."

Iris let her eyes drift shut. She ached for Torien's lost dreams and chances, for her shortened youth. She reeled from the depth of what Torien had shared, the insight it provided into this strong, honorable woman. Iris knew how modestly the Pacias family had grown up. Surely Tori resented her father...and felt guilty for doing so. How could she not harbor resentment for having had to relinquish a once-in-a-lifetime opportunity for college? How could she not feel guilty for the resentment? Iris couldn't even imagine. She bit her lip, studying Torien's serious profile. No wonder Torien took her responsibilities to heart. She'd learned the hard way how failing those you loved rippled through generations like a stone dropped in a pond. But it wasn't over. Torien's dreams weren't dead. "You can still go to college, you know," Iris said. "You're young."

"So are the twins, and they depend on me. *Mamá* as well. College doesn't matter for me. It's about them now."

"Well, yes, but—"

"Did you go to college, Iris?" Torien's expression was both wistful and...rife with challenge.

Iris paused, then shook her head, no longer ashamed of that fact. "I went to New York, Paris, Hong Kong, Rio, Milan, South Africa, Australia, London." She shrugged. "I started modeling when I was in high school, and when they want you, they want you. No rain check in modeling. Either you show up, or they find another pretty face."

"Was that your big dream, then? The modeling?"

Tilting her head side to side, Iris twisted her mouth and truly considered this. With Torien, no words were rambled, and no question was a toss-off. Iris's answer shouldn't be either. "It *was*. Back then."

"And now?"

Their gazes tangled for a moment, and Iris felt transparent as a dragonfly's wing. Her heart gave one big thud. What could she tell Torien about her dreams when she hardly had a grasp on them herself? The timer dinging cut through the moment, saving her the trouble of answering honestly. Thank God. Instead she raised her brows and said, "Now? I just want you to like my chicken."

Iris stood, but before she could enter the small *cabaña*, Torien grabbed her wrist and tugged her slightly off balance. Iris teetered, then landed with a whump on Torien's lap, facing her. Her sundress scrunched up at the hips, exposing a good portion of her thighs, well-tanned from all the time she'd spent in the gardens.

Surprised, Iris went still, drowning in those dark, haunted eyes. The heat of Torien's body warmed her inner thighs and throbbed at her center. She inadvertently tightened her legs around Torien's—pure feminine reflex.

Reflex or not, Torien didn't miss it. Pulling Iris closer, Tori's hands slid slowly around to span her waist, to caress her curves. Her thumbs traced the lines of Iris's rib cage. After a single breathless moment, Torien ran those hands up the length of Iris's back and eased her closer until Iris had to brace her hands on the wall at either side of Torien's head. Her hair fell forward in a sweep, strands of it resting on Torien's shoulder.

Torien searched Iris's face. "Thank you."

"For what?" Iris whispered, shaky with need.

"For…"

"Listening?" Iris suggested.

"No," Torien said, her voice a velvet rasp. "For *hearing*." She touched her lips to Iris's. Softly, gently. Tender and wine-flavored and wrapped in the drunk summer sweetness of honeysuckle in unrestrained bloom. Then once more, with a controlled jolt of urgency. Torien's tongue traced Iris's bottom lip, ending with a single nip that held a lifetime of promise.

Iris sighed into Torien's mouth, acutely aware of their breasts touching, tingling, aware of desire pooled, deep and throbbing in her body. Before she could recover from the dizzying onslaught of sensation, Torien pushed both of them up out of the chair and set Iris apart from her at arm's length.

Every vein, nerve, muscle in Iris's body screamed out for more. She blinked several times to regain what little composure she had around Tori. "Jesus, w-what was that for?"

Torien looked apologetic, flipping her hands over in an almost forlorn manner. "Forgive me. I simply did not wish for our first kiss to be blamed on a bet. Or the chicken."

First kiss.

Iris sure liked the sound of that.

The next several days working alongside Torien at the Círculo de Esperanza site flew by for Iris. Her buttermilk baked chicken was the talk of the worksite. Torien had loved it. Iris feigned nonchalance at the compliments and happily fulfilled requests for the recipe, but inside she lit up with pleasure. Easy, normal, everyday stuff, this.

As they worked, she stored up memories of laughter and deepening friendship, mud fights and wickedly hot, meaningful glances. Everyone seemed to accept that she and Torien shared something special, but no one probed for details or lobbed innuendo-laced comments their way. For that, she was grateful. Now that she'd earned Torien's friendship back—even shared a few kisses—Iris didn't want anything to scare her away. As Paloma had advised, Iris needed to crawl before she walked.

Instead of focusing on her growing feelings, Iris did her best to contribute to the never-ending work. She arrived early each morning, dug in immediately, and stayed until usually only she,

Madeira, and Torien remained. After eight days, she knew she had earned the respect of the other volunteers when Rubén, a man who had initially suffered from a bad case of idol worship and infatuation, had beckoned to her from the back of the truck, "*Oye*, Iris! Make yourself useful as well as ornamental. Grab the other end of this bench, will you?"

The other women working on the site had accepted her, too, shyly asking for makeup tips and probing for tales of her so-called exciting life all over the world.

She crawled home utterly exhausted each evening, blisters on her heels and calluses on her palms, but woke up feeling as though her days finally had meaning. Now, if only she could build a callus on her heart, she might be able to leave this world and honor her contractual obligations in Paris.

The day of reckoning rushed toward her like a prizefighter's right hook she couldn't quite block. *Paris.* Ostensibly, the City of Lights would be her home for the next three years. She had committed. She was expected. But not only was the thought of spending thirty-six months a continent away from Torien unbearable, the mere thought of heading to the airport was something she simply couldn't face. She had put off flight reservations and pushed the looming departure date out of her head, but finally she could avoid it no longer. She'd learned a lot about responsibility from Torien, and it was long past time to place the overseas call she dreaded.

One scant week before she was scheduled to fly out of Torien's life forever, she dialed Geraline's number in Milan with cold, shaking fingers. As the oddly unfamiliar telephone rings buzzed in her ear, her heart fought to break free of her rib cage. She paced to the edge of the stone terrace and leaned on the railing, staring at the gray, cloud-crowded sky as if it were the enemy. The regular spring thunderstorms had come to Colorado, and several more were expected over the next few days.

Come on. Answer.

The continual ring felt like a reprieve, and Iris released

a long, slow breath. She knew Gerri would be annoyed and scrambling once she heard Iris's request, but Gerri would do well to remember that she worked for Iris, not vice versa. Iris had promised herself she would take steps to change her life, and she meant to honor it. *As soon as Geraline answers the damn phone.*

Iris sighed.

Nothing like bolstering your courage for nothing.

Just as she was about to hang up, the call connected.

"Hello?"

She licked her dry lips, her body going rigid with tension. In a falsely jovial voice, she said, "Hi, Ger. It's me."

"Iris? What's wrong?"

"Nothing, I just wanted to check in." *Lie number one.* "Did I call at a bad time? I can't ever keep the time difference straight." *Lie number two.*

"No. I'm glad you called, actually. It saved me the dialing. Hang on a sec." Geraline sounded harried as ever. Iris heard her shuffle papers. "Okay, here it is. Fair warning, babe. Antoine will be in Denver sometime in the next week or so and I've told him he can stay at the house."

"That's fine," Iris said, distracted. Small talk was a good deflector when you wanted to drop a bomb on someone. "How'd his Klein shoot go?"

Static-crackled silence swept over the line. "'How did his Klein shoot go?' Wow, Iris. You were right. This vacation has done wonders for your attitude."

You have no idea, Iris thought.

"Whatever happened to, 'Gerri! He's a twit. How could you?'" she asked in a playful falsetto.

"I don't know." Iris smiled, filled with benevolence and peace. She wrapped one arm across her torso and rested her other elbow on it, then turned to lean her back on the railing. As if she'd been slapped, she was struck by how austere this Italianate mansion seemed when compared with the modest but love-filled homes in Círculo de Esperanza. Blatant displays of wealth had never been her vibe, sure. Her two indulgences had been her Mercedes roadster and the sprawling ranch house she had bought for her parents out near Brighton. "I guess I just… don't care one way or the other about Antoine. Anyway, listen, Gerri. The reason I called—"

"First, tell me you've gotten your plane ticket," Geraline said, all business, as usual.

Iris rolled her eyes. Tunnel vision. Money, money, money.

"Time's running out, you know. This time next week, you'll be in Paris."

Iris's heart clenched so painfully, it took concerted effort to sound casual and assertive at the same time. She tucked her hair behind her ear. "Actually…ah…that's why I called."

"What? What? Don't tell me something has happened."

"Gerri, chill. Nothing happened." She flailed her free arm out to the side in exasperation. "Let me *finish* a sentence, for God's sake!"

"Okay, I'm sorry. It's just that I have all these plates spinning in the air—"

"Same as usual," Iris deadpanned.

"You're right. I'm all ears. Go ahead."

It took Iris a moment to formulate her thoughts, and she uttered the words with her eyes squeezed shut, bracing herself against Geraline's explosion. "I need an extra month before I leave, Ger. I got involved with—"

"What? Iris! No. No way."

"Just listen to me for a minute," Iris countered, steely determined now that she'd jumped the first hurdle. "I've gotten involved with a really worthwhile volunteer project here and I don't want to leave it in the middle." *Lie number three.* Okay, so it was partially true. She did love her time working with the organization.

"Volunteer project? What? When?"

"It's called the Rainbow Project, but that doesn't matter.

Just hear me out." She sucked a deep breath for courage. "Those awful tabloid stories about me are still circulating. You've seen them, I assume?"

"Yes. So? Any publicity is good publicity. Get to the point."

Iris paced, increasingly psyched about her shoot-from-the-hip explanation the more she embellished. She supposed she could have mapped out this conversation beforehand, but no matter. The ad-libbed version was turning out to be divinely inspired. "Those articles cast an ugly shadow on my character. Working on this project will generate some good press to counteract the bad." When Geraline didn't argue, Iris surged forth. "You know how scathing the foreign press can be. I think the Jolie people would prefer to have a spokesperson known for donating her time to worthy causes rather than trading sexual favors for new boobs, don't you? Not that I actually did that," she added in a low, rapid tone.

"Fuck," Geraline snapped, punctuating it with a frustrated sigh.

Iris winced, then pressed the heel of her free hand to her forehead. "Please, Ger. I need this. I really—" An unexpected fist of emotion punched her in the throat, and she clamped her lips together to keep from begging. "I need a month."

Geraline's dubious sigh carried over the line. "One month?"

"Yes."

"I'll ask them, Iris. That's all I can do. I suppose they'll probably go for it. I mean, what choice do they have?"

Relief drained through Iris, so acute that it made her thighs shake. She wobbled to the chaise and sank into it, reclining. "Good. Thanks."

More shuffling of papers. "What did you say the name of that project was?"

"The Rainbow Project. *El Proyecto de Arco Iris* in Spanish."

"Oh, so it's like some cultural thing?"

A twinge of annoyance struck her, but she swallowed thickly. "A little ethnocentric, Ger, but I guess you could put it that way."

"Whatever. What's the whole point of it, anyway?"

Iris had to take three deep breaths before she could answer without sounding snippy. "It's mostly people from Mexico, building community gardens in disadvantaged neighborhoods," she added, in a monotone. Then, with more feeling, "Anyway, thanks, Gerri. This means a lot to me. More than you know."

"Okay." A pause. Iris heard Geraline tapping away at the computer keyboard. "How'd you get involved in this volunteer thing, anyway?" she asked, rather as an afterthought. "Last time I talked to you, you didn't have plans for your vacation."

Danger. Iris froze briefly, but recovered just as fast. "Yeah, I uh…they had a thing about it in the *Denver Post*. It sounded like a worthwhile way to spend my time."

"You're wearing sunscreen, I hope? Your skin needs to be impeccable."

"Of course." Iris's entire soul lifted, soared. A month. Four glorious weeks to get her head straight, to figure out the rest of her life. Four weeks with Torien. "Convince them I need the time, Ger."

"I'll do my best. You know I want to keep my favorite model happy."

Iris's laughter sounded tinny and forced in her ears. "I bet you say that to all your models."

Geraline chuckled, too. "Yeah, you know, I probably do. *C'est la vie.*" A small pause stretched. "You're sure nothing else has happened?"

"Positive." *Lie number four.* "Everything will be just fine." The rain started, and Iris closed her eyes and lifted her face to the cool, fresh glory of it.

New beginnings.

Wasn't that what Torien had said about rain?

CHAPTER EIGHT

It had been grueling work, but the day finally arrived when the garden at Círculo de Esperanza was finished. Wide expanses of dark, rich soil still showed beneath the newly set and spaced plants, but the volunteers were done. They just had to wait for Mother Nature to do her part to make the garden thrive, for the plants themselves to reach out to one another and cover the ground in a riot of color and life.

The community members had planned a celebration for the day after tomorrow, and the volunteers bustled about, cleaning, laughing, hugging—drunk on the pleasure of their massive accomplishment. From a trash-strewn dusty field to an apex of utter beauty, the true nucleus of an already tight neighborhood, and all because one woman—Torien—envisioned more for the wasted space.

As the long, golden fingers of late afternoon reached into the square, Madeira and Natán left to cart a load of refuse to the dump. Natán's wife, Judit, and her sister, Maria, relaxed on the curb, watching children drawing flowers on the sidewalk with chalk. Torien had gone into her house for a quick shower, and Iris crossed over to Torien's front stoop to indulge in a wide-angle view of their creation. She could scarcely believe the transformation.

A crisscross of slate stepping stones met in the middle of the square, where two half-moon wrought-iron and wood benches sat in a comfortable conversational grouping that the old men would love. Small dogwood trees, their fragile trunks braced with plastic-covered chains, set roots around the benches. The triangular garden areas between the paths contained carefully choreographed flowerbeds in a bevy of heights, textures, and colors. Lavender and pink creeping phlox contrasted with cheery white and yellow windflowers. Brilliant yellow goldenrod complemented the tall, fuzzy stalks of purplish gayfeather. Patches of daisies, sweet william, sneezewood, and Iris's favorite—purple coneflower—edged the entire magnificent array.

Iris's chest swelled with the kind of pride and pleasure she hadn't felt in years. They had cemented the community, energized the residents…with plants.

Plants, of all things.

And she had helped.

Sweat, tears, laughter, sore muscles—she had donated all of it.

Behind her, the door opened. Iris spun toward the sound. Torien stood on the other side of the screen, surprise widening her eyes. "Did you knock, Iris? I did not hear you."

"No." She wrapped her arms around her middle and absorbed the scents. The smell of early summer had always reminded her of biting into a fresh peach, and she loved the juicy trickle of it. Here in Torien's neighborhood, that aroma mingled with the familiar tang of steaming tamales wafting from one of the neighbors' kitchens. "I just wanted a bigger view of the garden."

The screen door creaked open and banged shut, and just like that, Torien stood next to her, shoulder to shoulder. Iris grew aware of Tori's warm hand at the small of her back just as she murmured, "It's beautiful, no?"

"Mmm." Iris's awareness shifted from the worksite to the dewy heat of the woman at her side. Tori looked different from how Iris was used to seeing her. Dampness clung to the edges of the clean hair at her neck. Torien had changed into a long-sleeved, faded *Life is Good* shirt with the sleeves shoved up to her elbows. Fitted, but not tight, dark wash Levi's and low-heeled black boots completed the casually alluring outfit. Torien's clothing carried that familiar sandalwood and bleach scent Iris had begun to associate with her, and she longed to bury her face in the soft folds of that shirt, the comfort of Tori's chest.

God, Torien was a devastatingly sexy woman, and she didn't even know it. *The dark wolf.* Smiling at that image, Iris faced her. "Thank you, Tori. For letting me work with you."

"De nada," Torien said, her tone a verbal caress. "You do good work." Her eyes traveled the curves of Iris's face, lingering on her eyes…and her lips. She reached out and smoothed a thumb along Iris's jawline. "I regret that I argued about you joining us in the first place."

"As well you should." Iris tugged the sleeve of Torien's shirt. Playfully at first, but the moment sobered, and, God help her, she couldn't let go. Didn't want to let go.

Ever.

As her pulse pounded in her ears, she stared at her fingers clutching Torien's sleeve until the image blurred before her eyes. Wanting her…wanting her…so badly she could cry. Slowly, Iris raised her face, aware of the quiver in her body. The ache that blinded her, that both weakened and strengthened her.

Torien noticed, too. *That look, that deepening, that promise.*

So quintessentially Tori.

Iris sensed the movement before it happened, or perhaps her soul's vehement wish manifested the entire moment. Regardless, Iris moved closer at the same time Tori slipped two fingers inside the waistband of Iris's denim shorts and closed the space between them. The lower halves of their bodies melded with an explosion of white-hot desire.

All at once, Torien's hands urgently cradled Iris's rib cage as their mouths met.

Iris sank into the kiss, as if pulling Torien's very essence inside was all she lived for, all she needed. Tori's face smelled of Caress soap and her tongue held a hint of mint toothpaste as it touched, pulled back, touched again. Nibbling, gently sucking. Warmth and heat and angel-wing sighs.

Hot, moist desire raged through Iris's body and a groan rumbled deep in her throat. She arched against Tori, the tips of her breasts hard and tingling beneath the tank top she wore. One of Tori's hands slid around to wind Iris's hair into a soft fist, the other splayed just below the small of her back. Tori braced her legs wide and pulled Iris into the welcoming circle of her body. Tugging her hair gently, Tori exposed Iris's neck to her mouth, raining kisses and nips until her lips met the strong beat of Iris's pulse. Tori moaned into the connection for a moment before flicking her tongue gently against the spot.

Giving in to the deep, rhythmic throb low in her body, Iris smoothed her fingers up Tori's sleeve and molded her hand around Tori's upper arm, caressing the bottom bulge of her toned biceps with her thumb. "Tori, I haven't showered," she whispered, her words slurred with desire. "I'm sweaty."

"I don't care, *mi ángel*," came the answer against her neck before Tori's lips traveled an urgent path to her jawline. "You taste like sunshine and heaven."

"The workers," Iris reminded her.

Tori stilled briefly, then without releasing Iris, without lifting her lips from Iris's skin, she fumbled behind her for the screen door handle, opening the door awkwardly and pulling Iris over the threshold. Their stumbling footsteps rang loudly against the tile entryway, but at last they were alone.

In the privacy of the house, Tori pushed Iris against the wall, arms above her head, their fingers intertwined. Tori slipped one hard thigh between Iris's. Urgent breaths heaved their breasts together, both soft and hard, tight and aching.

"Irisíta—"

"No." She shook her head. "Don't talk. Not now."

"I want—"

"I know," Iris whispered. "I want it, too, Tori. So much."

Passion-dark eyes traced Iris's face before Tori's taut, lean body moved against Iris's in a rhythm that could only be called a prelude of lovemaking. Tori's mouth captured Iris's once again, one deep kiss before she bent to kiss her way down Iris's trembling body. Tori's fingers slipped from Iris's grasp, palms smoothing down the insides of her arms, over the curves and hollows to the sides of her breasts. Tori's thumbs brushed over her nipples once. Again.

Iris groaned.

They brushed again, more urgently, and Iris arched into the caress. Wanting more, her fingers, her mouth, everything Tori had to give. Iris's nerves were so shot with desire, her skin hummed. Tori reached one hand up and under Iris's tank top, shoving it aside, and then her teeth sank gently into the flat softness of Iris's stomach. Iris moaned, wanting to die from the pleasure, from the visceral gush of need, the deep, aching throb at her center. Tori had to touch her, taste her, be inside her or she would die.

Right here. Right now.

Skin on skin, closer than close. Iris clutched Torien's shoulder, pulling her up. "Tori, please—"

Tori stood, body covering Iris's again, melding, moving, rocking to the rhythm of that hot, moist throb. She pressed kisses against Iris's face, nose, eyelids, all the while crooning, "*Quiero estar contigo*, Irisíta. I need to be inside you."

"Yes."

"Deep inside."

"Please…"

"You want that?"

"God…yes."

"So sweet, baby. So hot," Tori murmured against her skin. Her hand slid down to cup the heat between Iris's legs, moving the heel of her hand in slow, agonizing circles. "Are you wet for me, *querida*? Do you want me here?"

"Please, yes. Tori—"

"Quiero hacerte el amor."

"Yes," Iris whispered, what had to be a thousand times or more, gasping for air in between the gentle dominance of Tori's mouth, the vibrating caress of love words against her heated skin, the promising pressure of her palm.

Just when Iris thought she would go crazy from the ardent demands of Tori's hand, the screen door creaked. Loud, rapid Spanish froze the moment with all the grace of a bucket of slush being dumped over their heads.

They wrenched apart just as Madeira burst in with all the grace of a teenager, slamming the door back against the wall and calling, "Tor—" Her eyes widened, moving from Torien to Iris and back. "Ohh," she finished lamely. "Whoops."

Embarrassed, Iris lowered her head, the back of her hand lifting to her lips, smoothing away the passion that lingered there. Anxious hands, straightening clothes, clasping behind her back. She adored Madeira, but damn if her timing wasn't the absolute worst.

"I…I'm sorry," Madeira said. "I didn't know—"

"It's okay," both Iris and Torien said.

Torien shoved her hands through her hair and released a frustrated sigh. "What do you need, Mosquito?" she asked, her tone low.

Madeira looked as though she were trying her best to pretend she had no clue what she'd interrupted, but the raging pheromones in the entryway told a different story. "Ah…yeah. So, the rest of us are going down to El Tío Feo for a beer to celebrate finishing the garden." Madeira aimed a thumb over her shoulder. "Are… you two planning to join us, or…?"

Torien glanced at Iris, her eyes dark and wanting and intimate. The unspoken message conveyed that one word from Iris, and Madeira would be gone. She and Tori would be making love…mind, body, soul…in a matter of minutes. "It's up to you, Irisíta."

Iris blinked several times, wanting Tori so badly but knowing they must do the right thing. Hadn't she learned that from Torien herself? She pulled the corner of her mouth in between her teeth and swallowed back bitter regret. "We should go, Tori. Celebrate with the others."

Torien's lips, still moist and swollen with passion, pressed into a flat line. She jerked a single nod, her eyes never leaving Iris's face as she told Madeira, "We'll go." She scrubbed the palm of her hand over her eyes. "Just—"

"Give us a minute, Madi," Iris finished, with a smile.

"No. I-I understand. Take your time. See you there." And Madeira was gone.

Iris sagged against the wall. "Damnit."

"Yeah." Torien braced one arm above Iris, face mere inches from hers. With a groan, Torien rested her forehead against Iris's. The ticking clock in the kitchen was the first thing Iris noticed as her body returned to normal. After that, the sounds of children playing outside, the laughter of the workers, the pounding, pounding, pounding of her heart. She licked her lips, and Torien's head lifted, gaze dropping to drink in the motion.

Tori reached out and trailed one finger from Iris's throat, down her chest to her waistband and back up.

"I have to go home and shower," Iris whispered.

"You can shower here."

"I don't have a change of clothes."

"Okay."

"I won't be long."

"Take your time."

A pause, thick with regret, ensued. Iris swallowed, watching a newly tormented Torien suck in one side of her cheek. Those eyes looked so intense, so focused, so...unreadable.

"C-can you pick me up? I don't know where the bar is."

"Of course."

"Tori?" Another pause.

"Yes?"

"I know that was bad timing and all, but…this…isn't over, is it?"

A huff of soft laughter. "Ah, sweet Irisíta." Torien touched Iris's chin, her bottom lip, the line of her collarbone. Her eyes flamed with a richness of feeling Iris had never before experienced outside of her dreams. *"Mi amor,"* Torien murmured, moving her body against Iris's once more, "this hasn't even begun."

❖

The drive from Circle of Hope to Geraline's mansion in the exclusive Denver Country Club area was deceptively short, though the drastic contrast between the two areas could not be ignored. Where Torien's community fairly undulated with life and music and people, Gerri's was closed up, fenced off, gated, and austere.

One said, *Look at what I own.*

The other said, *This is who we are.*

They didn't talk much on the drive. Iris spent the time reliving the silken beauty of Torien's mouth and hands on her body. If the look on Torien's face was any indication, she was thinking the same. They made plans to meet in the gazebo and go from there. Iris ran through the gardens and bustled into the house, in a rush to get ready for the evening out with the workers. To get *through* the evening and back into Torien's arms was closer to the truth. She kicked off her mud-encrusted shoes in the foyer and started up the stairs, but something stopped her.

On impulse, she hurried through the house to the stone terrace, throwing open the French doors and smiling when the rain-heavy breeze lifted her hair away from her face. She padded to the railing and leaned over, scouting the gardens for Torien, and caught sight of her rounding the potter's cottage with a cutting of roses, same as the first day she had seen her. Iris's tummy clenched with an odd sort of déjà vu. She straightened, the image blurring before her.

Not so long ago, she had no idea what she wanted to do with the rest of her life. Helping to create the beautiful little garden in Círculo de Esperanza was the first thing she'd done in a long time that left her flush with the pleasure of accomplishment. Now, with her muscles sore from honest work and her heart filled with the easy love and simplicity rife in Torien's world, she knew exactly what she wanted from her own life.

A real home.

A woman who loved her.

Fresh vegetables she had grown herself in her own private garden.

The time and space to build a future.

Waking up early just to make love. Again.

Obscurity, normalcy.

Torien.

She wanted…Torien.

The pure truth of it staggered her. Iris's heart simply wasn't in Paris anymore, and it never would be. The truth was so clear now, she could hardly believe she hadn't seen it weeks ago. Feeling wobbly and nervous inside, she knew what she had to do, and soon. It would likely damage her career forever—or end it—but she didn't care.

She *had* to break the contract with Jolie.

In the grander scheme of things, the career fallout wouldn't matter much because, frankly, she didn't want to model anymore. She was thirty. Wealthy. Ready to move on to something else in life, something far more fulfilling. Iris knew she wouldn't be missed for long. There would always be another pouty-lipped teen sensation to take her place.

A sense of peace cooled her body and soothed her soul. This was right. She felt it in her solar plexus—heart center. Of course, she wouldn't dump the entire story on Torien until things settled between them. She frankly didn't know if Torien shared her dream of a future together, and more than anything, Iris didn't want to spook her. If things worked out as planned, Torien would find out about her career change soon enough.

Filled with glee and a buoying sense of freedom, Iris waved her arms to get Torien's attention. "Tori!" she called out, smiling when the great love of her life glanced up.

She waved—cool, casual—then blew Iris a kiss.

"Forty minutes," Iris said, flashing ten fingers, four times.

"I will be waiting," Torien replied.

Her stomach in a swirl of anticipation, she turned from the railing and came face-to-face with Antoine…and Geraline. Iris gasped, splaying her hand on her chest. Time slowed and warped, as it often does when two worlds collide. Bad special effects in an even worse movie. Antoine she'd sort of expected. But what in the hell was Geraline doing there? Iris managed to clear her throat enough to speak. "God, you guys scared me."

Antoine smirked, but she ignored him, turning her attention instead to her business manager. A caged bird of panic beat wings inside her stomach. She felt like a teenager who got busted doing something wrong…even though it wasn't wrong at all.

The shrapnel, though…

Had Gerri witnessed her exchange with Torien? Though Iris wanted to take out a full-page ad in the *New York Times* proclaiming her love for Torien, she knew how Gerri felt about "the help" mingling with her houseguests. Iris might be bursting with the news, with the sheer, aching beauty of it all, but what would it all mean for Torien? She went for a casual slant. "Ger, I-I didn't know you were coming."

"Yes, well. I decided it would be in my best interests to come home and escort you to Paris myself." Her eyes narrowed, but she feigned a casualness Iris knew in the pit of her stomach Gerri didn't feel. "You didn't seem exactly eager to go."

Antoine stretched his neck to see around her. "Who's Tori?"

Iris's heart revved, and she flipped her hand like it couldn't have mattered less. "Huh? Oh, no one. Geraline's gardener." Then, to Geraline, "I told you. I was working on the volunteer project—"

"But you conveniently forgot to tell me you were working with my employee." A pointed pause. "Didn't you?"

Iris's throat went dry.

"It took me a while to make the connection, but you see, I trusted Pacias enough to loan her some gardening equipment for her little project. I didn't think she'd consider you part of that bargain."

Desperation clawed wildly at Iris.

No. *No, no, no!*

She couldn't bear to see something as pure and positive as her relationship with Tori tainted by ugly innuendo, by Torien possibly losing her job. Not now. "It's not like that, Gerri. Besides, what does it matter how I found out about the project?"

"It probably wouldn't, if that was all it was. But we just saw the woman blowing you a kiss, Iris, and I'm no idiot." Geraline tossed her silver sweep of hair, shook her head, and expelled a sigh of disappointment. "What were you thinking? Pacias is a common laborer, for God's sake. She barely speaks English."

Rage exploded in Iris's chest. "Her English is perfect."

Gerri ignored that. "You're a supermodel, Iris. A celebrity, with an image to maintain. If you insist on this whole lesbian thing, you could have any woman you want."

And I want Torien, Iris thought.

"The gardener. Dude, way to slum. Sounds like one of those books I wouldn't read—"

"As if you can read," Iris snapped.

"Interesting, though," Antoine drew out. "You two got some kind of a Cinderella thing going on?"

Iris rolled her eyes as best she could. "Don't be an asshole, Antoine. Torien helped me get my car to the dealership for service and I...I was showing my gratitude."

"Kids! No fighting." Gerri paused until the two of them had retreated into separate corners, metaphorically speaking. "Iris, Iris, Iris," Geraline intoned, pacing slowly to the opposite end of the terrace. She braced her bejeweled fingers on the railing for a moment, then turned. "I'm shocked you'd think I'm so obtuse. Truly. Shocked."

"Listen," Iris implored, moving toward Geraline. "Don't take this out on Torien. She didn't do anything wrong. She didn't even want me to work on the project, but I forced it. I forced her to let me hang around, and because she respects you, respects how you want her to treat your guests, she acquiesced. Plus, the project is done now."

Geraline's right eyebrow arched. "So what's happening in forty minutes, then?"

Iris toyed briefly with lying, but decided against it. She hadn't done well fabricating stories so far. "I'm just going to celebrate finishing the garden with the other volunteers, that's all. It's like a wrap party." She needed a little time with Torien, a chance to explain, to warn her about a possible impending storm.

Slate skies.

Flipped leaves.

The rumble of Gerri's thunder.

Iris flicked a glance at the giant marble wall clock. "I have to get ready and…Torien's going to drive me there because I don't know the way. Please, Ger—"

"Fine, Iris. I'm well-versed in the whims of…your type."

What?

"Go get ready for your little celebration with the hired help. But we're going to talk later," Geraline said. "And I'm not happy."

Little celebration?

Hired help?

Your type?

What the fuck was that all about? If Iris hadn't been sure of her decision before, this conversation solidified it. Fuming,

Iris fought to hide it. She clasped her hands together in front of her and forced an encouraging smile around her clenched jaw. "I know you aren't, Gerri, but it will work out for the best for all of us, I promise. I won't be too late. And we'll talk it out when I get back." *You had better bet we'll talk it out later.*

Have it out was more like it…

❖

Footsteps. Torien glanced up from the most current issue of *La Crónica de Hoy*, which she had been reading in the gazebo while she waited for Iris. She smiled, anticipating her first glimpse, but instead a baby-faced *hombre rubio* sauntered up the steps. His clothing looked arrogantly expensive, out of place in the gardens, and his attitude matched. But beneath the bluster, the boy had mean eyes and a weak chin. Not to mention, he was far too pretty for his own good—and that wasn't a compliment.

Stuffing the newspaper aside, Torien stood, no longer smiling and not even wanting to. Something in her gut put her immediately on guard. *"Buenas tardes, señor."*

"Hey," the man replied. "You Tori, the gardener?"

The man made it sound like an insult. "I am Torien Pacias, *sí.*" Wait a minute. This was the man from the *terraza*, that first night when she'd met Iris. Torien vaguely remembered that Iris didn't seem to like him, and if first impressions meant anything, she didn't blame her a bit. "May I help you with something?"

"You? Nah. I'll probably be staying here now and then." He raked Torien with a scathing glance. "I just wanted to meet some of Geraline's servants."

Torien struggled not to bristle at the term.

"I'm Antoine," he said, pausing as though Torien should recognize him.

No such luck.

He bugged his eyes, waiting.

She remained still.

"Hello, the model?" he added impatiently, flipping his soft hand as though the details of his life should be common knowledge.

Torien's gaze dropped briefly to the man's mixed drink, then back up. Perhaps he was only this obnoxious when he got *borracho*. Torien did not quite know what sort of response Antoine expected after this announcement of his apparently illustrious career.

"Surely you've seen my pictures. They're everywhere."

"Yes. I am certain I have," Torien lied.

"Right. Well, I'm more difficult to recognize with all my clothes on, maybe."

Torien fantasized about dumping a bag of manure over his head.

Antoine strutted around the gazebo with long, slow strides, his hard-soled Italian leather shoes echoing on the wooden floor. Finally, he sat on the bench across from Torien, legs spread wide, cunning eyes narrowed and watching over the rim of the glass as he drank. The ice against the crystal jangled unusually loud.

Torien sat, too, but cautiously. This man had an agenda. Until she found out what it was, her guard was up.

After swallowing and wiping his lips against the back of his hand, Antoine asked, "Shouldn't you be…gardening or something?"

The implication was clear. This cocky *hombre afeminado* might as well have come right out and accused her of neglecting her work. Torien itched to punch him in the face for the unfair accusation, but of course, she held back. The idiot was a guest of *Señora* Moreno, which afforded him a measure of respect whether he deserved it or not.

"I am finished with my work for the day," she managed not to snap, wishing to add that it was none of his goddamned business. Torien tried for casual, but her words still came out with an undercurrent of snide. "*Señora* Moreno lets her *servants* have their own lives, too."

"Mmm. Big of her. So, why are you still here?"

Torien jerked her chin toward the *cabaña* that held so many good memories now that Iris had come along. "I live here."

"Yeah?" Antoine lurched around and swept a disinterested glance over the small structure. "Huh. I thought that was a storage shed. Better than the back of a truck, though, eh?"

Rage shot through Torien. *How dare this asshole assume—* Enough. She had taken all she could stand from this man. *Boy,* she amended. A petulant, imbecile child. Torien stood, nodding as politely as she could manage. "Excuse me." She started down the steps, intending to wait for Iris on the porch of her *cabaña*, but the man's statement stopped her.

"She's good, isn't she?" Antoine called out.

Everything inside Torien's body went ice cold. Slowly... ever so slowly so as not to lash out, Torien faced him. The pulse at her neck pounded, anger rushed in her ears. "Pardon me?"

"Iris. Sweet...hot...Iris." He swirled the ice clockwise, then counterclockwise. Languid. Calculating. "Bet you've never been inside something that rich before." Flat eyes raised slowly, taunting.

Torien's hands wound into fists. "Watch your mouth."

"Perhaps you should watch yours, *Tori.* Where you're putting it, that is." He drained the glass. "Geraline Moreno is a powerful woman. She doesn't like her models to tramp around with the illegal household help."

Something inside Torien snapped, and the picture before her blazed red as though in flames. She would not listen to anyone speak of Iris as if she were a common street whore. Antoine could assume whatever he wished about "the illegal household help," but when he dragged Iris into it, that was the breaking point. "You're a weak, pathetic liar. Iris would never be with a boy like you."

"Yeah? You think she would rather be with *you*? The goddamned gardener?" He leaned his head back and laughed, the action seeming choreographed and false, like everything else about him. "Big damn dreams, eh, *amigo?* Face it. You never will fit in our world. Iris knows it. I know it. And you've known it all along, haven't you, *Tori?*"

Torien's bravado faltered.

Antoine smirked. "Iris might want a little piece, like a tacky souvenir to remind her of vacation. But she belongs in the limelight, not stuck with you." His tone went from snide to threatening, just like that. "You're just holding her back."

The shake started in the pit of her stomach and worked its way out toward her extremities. "Get the fuck out of my gardens," Torien growled.

Antoine gaped as though watching the antics of a child. "Your gardens?" He glanced around dismissively. "Let me tell you something, Juanita Valdez. You might pull the weeds here, but this little flower patch belongs more to me than it will ever belong to you, and don't you forget it."

"Go to hell," Torien bit out.

"Now, come on." He raised his arms in a gesture of surrender, but something vengeful and bitter shone in the cold ice of his hollow blue eyes. "I'm just trying to do you a favor, save you some embarrassment before Moreno gets hold of you." A beat passed. "She's here, you know," Antoine added casually.

Torien's stomach lurched and she flicked a glance at the big house, surprisingly caught off guard. Was *Señora* Moreno really here? Why?

"But say no more," Antoine continued. "You want me out of *your* gardens, I'm gone. I'll be sure to tell Geraline what a… nice job you've done with her…property." He set the crystal bar glass sharply on the polished teak bench, stood, then flicked a manicured hand toward it. "Take care of that for me before you leave. Will you, *amiga?*"

CHAPTER NINE

A popular dance band from Corpus Christi pumped cumbia rhythms through the familiar darkness of El Tío Feo. Bass reverberated across the polished wooden floor and up through the metal legs of Torien's chair as she sat with the others around two long tables shoved together.

The club, which had been empty when they arrived two hours earlier, had filled with women. Tucked away in a semi-private corner and oblivious to the other patrons, the volunteers sipped beers and shared loud laughter and exaggerated stories. Torien could see in their eyes how proud they were for having once again accomplished something many skeptics had said was impossible. The Círculo de Esperanza site marked their fifth success without steady funding, and all the gardens were thriving. Once the group had finished, each neighborhood took on the responsibility for upkeep of the garden as if it were one of the local children, theirs to nurture.

Torien shared the group's sense of achievement, but couldn't muster enthusiasm to match, nor could she focus on their celebration. She was there in body, but not in mind or spirit, thanks to the confrontation with that asshole, Antoine. Blinding fury had slowly given way to sobering resignation. In many ways, much as she hated to admit it, Antoine was right.

Iris Lujan had merged into Torien's world just fine. Everyone had warmed to her immediately and Madeira was clearly half in love with Iris herself. *Sí*, Iris fit so perfectly it was as if Torien's life were a nearly finished picture puzzle with Iris as the only missing piece.

She fit. But she didn't *belong*.

Her presence was like an unexpected visit from an angel. Something to be enjoyed fleetingly and tucked away as a memory. Iris had a great big life outside their little insular world, a fact everybody except Torien seemed unwilling to face. Torien, however, had no other choice but to face it, because like an idiot, she had gone and fallen in love with Iris. And just as Antoine had pointed out so harshly, Torien should never have fooled herself into believing this could be more than a once-in-a-lifetime affair with one of the most world-famous Chicana models.

Torien had tried to protect herself against wanting more, but sweet Iris simply…inspired love. She was a white light that drew people to her, surely as moths to a bulb, and Torien had dropped her guard and been sucked in by the glow. No big surprise. Half the world was in love with Iris Lujan. Torien? Merely one of many.

But last time she checked, "Tortilla Flats" was short on world-class modeling agencies and cosmetic empires. Though Antoine had stated it more cruelly than necessary, Torien knew she had nothing to offer Iris Lujan.

Nothing.

Once Moreno learned of their inappropriate relationship, none of it would matter anyway. Torien would always be grateful they had become friends, flattered that Iris had extended her vacation in order to help them finish the garden. But her time here was *still* nothing more than a vacation from her real life. Torien knew, eventually, Iris would go, leaving the puzzle of her own crazy life unfinished forever.

Why was she the only one willing to admit that?

With any other woman, Torien might welcome the brief distraction, but a sane woman did not love Iris Lujan and then simply move on to someone else. Ridiculous. Yet Torien's gut told her she *had* to move on. Not to another woman, but on with her life.

So...she would not have Iris.

Small sacrifice to save her own soul, she supposed.

Thank God Madeira had interrupted them when she had. Making love to Iris would have been a fatal error. Letting her go, period, would be hard enough. Already, the taste of her skin, the sound of her passion, were branded upon Torien's brain. If she ever managed to erase the sensual images, it would be a miracle. But if they'd made love, ridding her mind of Iris would destroy Torien with its impossibility.

She clutched her beer bottle, wanting to be angry with herself, but too depressed to pull off any emotion more passionate than listlessness. The fight-or-flight instinct kicked in with a vengeance, and she wanted to leave the bar. Escape her pain. Run *from* Iris before she ran *to* her.

You were a damned fool for thinking it could last, Toro.

Judít finished a joke she'd been telling and the table erupted into laughter. Iris's hair—smelling of coconuts and sunlight, sleek as satin—brushed Torien's arm as she bent her head forward to laugh. Iris wore loose-fitting jeans, a silky black tank top, and flat black sandals. Her slim fingers were twined around the neck of the brown beer bottle from which she had peeled the label, inordinately proud because it had come off in one piece. Her eyes had sparkled when she held it up for Torien to see.

The entire tableau appeared so damn normal—deceptively so.

Two women.

A bar.

Desire.

But it wasn't normal. It was a lie. All of it except the love she felt for Iris, the crushing desperation when she thought about losing her.

Inevitable.

Feigning nonchalance she did not feel, Torien hooked the beer bottle between her fingers and lifted it to her mouth. Taking a deep swallow, she watched Iris's reflection in the mirrored wall. The yellow and red bar lights danced over her features, burning instantaneous erotic images in Torien's mind. Her body responded almost violently. She closed her eyes for a moment of silent self-reproach. This was Iris Lujan, for God's sake. What was she doing with Torien at a ratty little local bar in *el barrio*?

Enough! Her bottle hit the table with a sharp clunk.

All at once, Iris's lovely wide eyes lifted to the mirror, meeting Torien's in the reflection. The snapshot moment was too ironic to ignore. Two women from different worlds, staring ahead, not at each other. They walked parallel paths through a life that had crossed by sheer accident, not some destined twist of fate. Couldn't Iris see that?

Clearly not. Her full lips curved slowly upward, lighting her luminous green eyes with the warmth of promise. Iris turned from the mirror to face Torien for real. Torien kept her gaze trained on the mirror, memorizing the soft, feminine angles of Iris's profile, the proud nose, the sensual long line of her neck.

"Hey," Iris said. Low. Intimate.

Torien felt the soft puff of breath against her jaw. She forced herself to face the woman she loved…her lovely flesh-and-blood Iris. *My dark garden angel, come to life.*

For a long moment, Iris searched Torien's face, as if to ferret out clues about her silence. Before Torien knew what had happened, Iris ducked forward almost shyly and nipped at Torien's bottom lip with her teeth, finishing with one small caress of her tongue.

Torien stiffened and lurched back, heartbeat rough, painful, like jagged glass.

"Is everything okay?"

"Fine."

"We haven't even had a chance to talk yet and…we really should talk." Shadows moved across Iris's expression.

Bleak resolution sank in Torien's gut. Moreno was back, real life beckoned its crooked, demanding finger. This…fantasy between the two of them was truly over.

A small frown dimmed the light in Iris's eyes. "Tori, what's wrong?"

Torien's mind warred with what to say, what would be easiest? The kindest? Truth, Torien decided. Painful, yes, but the easiest route. "I don't know," she said carefully.

Iris pulled her chin back. "That doesn't sound promising."

"I know. It isn't."

"Honey, sometimes you are too honest for your own good."

No answer.

"I'm just kidding." Iris tucked her hair behind her ear and jostled against Torien's shoulder. When Torien remained mute, Iris's expression sobered. "Okay, now I'm worried. What's weighing so heavily on your mind?"

Torien huffed, shaking her head and staring glumly into the mouth of her beer bottle. "Why do women always ask that question?"

"I guess because we want to know. Besides, you're a woman, too, albeit the strong and silent type." Iris's tone came off light, but Torien could feel the undercurrent of worry beneath her words. "Truthfully, I've come to realize the only way to get inside your head is to ask, since you sure aren't one for offering the information." She was teasing.

Still, Torien couldn't form words around the tightness in her throat. A long, uncomfortable moment yawned through the chasm separating them.

"*Hey*. Talk to me."

Torien met those green eyes directly. "Sometimes it is better not to know what a silent woman is thinking."

All vestiges of humor and passion dropped from Iris's face. "Something happened."

Sí, Irisíta. I have fallen in love with a woman I cannot have. Not forever and not completely. So not at all.

"No. I…" Torien scrubbed a palm over her face, buying time, strengthening her resolve. "The long days are catching up with me."

The fire of intimacy returned. Iris leaned in, her tone like a cat's pleasured purr. "Take me home and I guarantee I'll make you forget how tired you are." A pause. "Then we'll talk."

Tacky little souvenir.

Despite the ugly image, desire pierced Torien like an arrow and she could not steel herself against the assault. She couldn't seem to escape the images of that afternoon, the tactile memory of Iris's breasts pressed against hers, her hands spanning Iris's rib cage as if they had done so a thousand times before…would do so a million times again. Forbidden softness, so sweet and lovely. The scent of need clinging to her skin as she'd moved against Iris, the taste and heat of her flesh, the rumble of her moans.

Torien was no Madeira, but she had enjoyed her fair share of women. Despite her sister's taunts, she had no desire to attain sainthood when it came to such pleasures. But this afternoon with Iris had been different. Torien hadn't yearned to possess Iris, to partake of her body like a hungry woman faced with a full feast. She had ached to connect. To show Iris with her body what she failed so miserably to say with mere words.

Torien wanted to love her.

Wanted to express her love in the only way she felt fully capable.

But she didn't want to make love to Iris only to bid her goodbye. Torien didn't wish to be anyone's tacky little souvenir, but especially not Iris's. She didn't think she could survive that kind of pain.

Fool.

Idiot.

"Tori?" Iris's warm palm on her arm, soft words, loving eyes. "Honey, talk to me."

"No. I cannot—" Antoine's scathing words rushed back at her like whispering demons.

Servant.

You will never fit in our world…Iris knows it, too.

Fueled to escape from her own weak will and nurse her wounded pride, Torien shot to her feet, inadvertently overturning her chair. The metal back of it bounced on the hard floor twice before coming to a rest, and the table quieted, all faces turning toward her curiously. She looked at Iris, filled with urgency. "Stay with Madeira, Irisíta, okay?"

"Stay with—what do you mean?" Iris stammered, confused and stunned.

Stiffly, Torien stooped and righted the chair, then sought the face of her sister. "*Oye.*" Torien lifted her chin slightly. "Drive Iris home when she is ready, *sí*?" she shoved her hands through her hair. "I must…go."

Madeira frowned. "Toro?"

"Wait—" Iris grabbed at her sleeve but Torien shook gently from her grasp.

"I am sorry. I…do not feel well." At least it wasn't a lie. Before anyone could stop her, Torien zigzagged through the crowds, heedless of the people she bumped into, knowing only she had to get away.

Run.

Fast and far.

Hide from the truth.

She grew aware of the startled murmurs sweeping through the bar in her wake. They built to an excited crescendo similar to the day Iris had first arrived at the Círculo de Esperanza worksite. Torien yanked open the door, but stopped, gripping its edge. Something compelled her to turn back toward the commotion, knowing what she would see, needing to drink in the image of Iris one more time. But she was wholly unprepared for the hurt and bewilderment in Iris's eyes.

A sick feeling dropped like wet gravel in her stomach. Iris stood in the middle of the bar, a throng of excited women— fans—who'd clearly just realized they had a superstar in their midst surrounded her. Arms jostled and grabbed at her, but she was oblivious. Her moist, questioning gaze locked firmly with Torien's, seeing only her, as if nothing else existed.

"Wait," Torien saw Iris mouth.

Torien shook her head. Guilt grappled with self-preservation, and self-preservation won. Iris's adoring public encircling her underscored Antoine's vicious point about the basic incompatibility of their lives.

Madeira shouldered her way through the throng and bustled up beside Torien, grabbing her arm. *"¿Qué pasó?"* Open astonishment tinged Madeira's question. "What happened? Where the hell are you going?"

"I can't—" Torien flicked a quick glance at Madeira before reconnecting her gaze with Iris. Torien's lips pressed together, holding back her torment. "Listen, stay with her. Do that for me."

Madeira frowned, her tone raised to be heard above the ruckus. "Why aren't *you* staying with her?"

"Not now, Mosquito, I beg you." She wrangled her arm away. "I have to go. Let me—"

"But—"

"Don't leave her alone in here," Torien implored. "Take her home and see her inside. Please. Do this one thing for me, and I'll explain later."

"Toro, if you can just tell me—"

"Say it," she rasped. She clutched Madeira's shoulder, shaking it slightly. "Say you will not leave her. Promise me."

"Of course I won't. But—"

"And tell her…tell her I am sorry." Torien turned.

"Toro!"

Ignoring her sister's plea, Torien stepped into the cool, wet, storm-whipped night and let the door close behind her.

❖

Shoving through the crowds, Iris forced her way to the front door and threw it open just in time to see the taillights of Torien's truck flicker when the engine turned over. A short plume of exhaust shot from the tailpipe, and then the reverse lights glared white and bright through the inky night.

Iris splashed across the wet blacktop toward the truck, panic pummeling her brain like a hailstorm. She couldn't let Torien just run away. The rain completely soaked her feet through her sandals, and already, her silk tank top clung to her skin. She didn't care about any of it, anything except reaching Torien. Geraline was back, and the little safe cocoon she had built with Torien would undoubtedly change forever. Instinct told Iris if Torien escaped her this time, she wouldn't get her back.

Tires squealed as Torien backed out, and Iris heard the gears grind from reverse to drive. "Tori! Stop!" Iris yelled. The wind threw it back at her.

Torien didn't stop.

And, just like that, she was gone.

Torien didn't know how long she had been driving, nor did she care. The miles and miles of pavement running beneath her truck gave her time to think, and in doing so, she had reached one conclusion.

She loved Iris.

And Iris deserved to know that before things between them ended. Torien knew she shouldn't have bolted, but it couldn't be helped. She would face Iris. Apologize.

But first, she had to face Moreno.

She pulled up to the *cabaña* and parked, sitting for a minute just listening to the rain on the metal roof. She wasn't sure what exactly Moreno knew about her and Iris, but she owed the woman an explanation. Moreno had trusted her, and even knowing the rules, agreeing with the rules, Torien had breached them. She'd tried to avoid Iris, to avoid the deep, growing feelings, but she had failed. So be it. She'd resigned herself to the mistake. But to deny her love for Iris would cheapen their relationship, and she wasn't willing to stoop so low. Moreno was a reasonable woman. Torien felt sure she would understand, and if not…well, Torien had survived crushing disappointment before.

Exiting the car, she tucked her face against the rain and trotted toward the *cabaña*, only realizing Moreno sat there in the darkness when she caught the scent of the heavy, expensive perfume the woman favored.

Torien stopped short, smoothing the rain from her shoulders and hair. "*Señora*. Welcome home."

"Good to be here."

Several beats passed.

"Are you…waiting for me?"

Moreno studied her for a moment, expression unreadable. She seemed to roll the response around in her mouth, and her mind. "I am, Ms. Pacias." She glanced around. "The gardens look splendid. Your work is impeccable."

Wary, yet hopeful after the compliment, Torien tentatively took a seat next to Moreno. She supposed her employer heard about the earlier run-in with Antoine. Another transgression for which she owed an apology, though that one would be difficult at best to make. "Thank you."

As though reading her mind, Moreno said, "Antoine told me you two…had words this afternoon."

"*Sí*. I apologize, *señora*, but he said some derogatory things about *Señora* Lujan that—"

"Ah, yes. Our Iris. That's the real issue here, isn't it?" Geraline waved her hand. "Don't worry about Antoine. He's young. He talks too much, especially when he's drinking."

A small measure of relief poured through Torien.

"But Iris…" Geraline paused, assessing Torien through

narrowed eyes as she tapped her fingers on her lips. "That's a problem we need to discuss."

The statement stole Torien's breath.

Moreno was not pleased. Torien felt the tension crackle in the air like lightning. At a total loss, she said the only thing that came to mind: the truth.

"I love her."

The words hung between them like a noose, the perfect size for her neck. Torien waited, poisonous dread coursing through her veins.

Moreno did not appear impressed by the declaration. On the contrary, her disgust was nearly tangible. Her tone, however, remained well-modulated, like that of a woman who knew she held all the cards. "Do you have…*any idea* who she is?"

"Of course."

Moreno ran her hands through her hair without seeming to move a single perfect strand. Her voice dropped an octave, to something dangerous. "I thought I had made it clear when I left that you should keep to your own business."

"You did." Torien held steady. "I…tried."

Moreno snorted and shook her head. "You're saying Iris caused all the problems?"

"Absolutely not."

"Then what?"

"She came to the gardens crying one night, and I spoke to her out of concern. From there"—she shrugged—"things just happened."

"Things don't just *happen*, Torien. Someone is to blame here."

Torien stiffened. That's what this was about? "Then blame me. Not Iris."

Moreno shot to her feet and stalked a few short paces to the end of the porch, grabbing the pole that supported the roof. After a moment, she turned. "She did tell you about Paris, I assume?"

Paris? Torien flailed to keep the shock and bewilderment from seeping into her expression, but from the gleam of victory in Moreno's eyes, Torien knew she'd failed.

"Ah...I see," Geraline drawled, with a smile. "Our little Iris wanted to have a fling, and she picked you as the likely target. It all makes sense now."

"What about Paris?"

"She's leaving for Paris next week. She has a three-year modeling contract there. If she didn't tell you"—Moreno huffed—"then clearly your intentions are more honorable than hers."

Torien shook her head, the motion wooden.

Paris?

No. Unthinkable.

Why hadn't Iris mentioned it?

Why had she allowed Torien to fall in love with her when she knew it could go nowhere?

Moreno spread her arms. "So, you see? The whole thing is one-sided anyway."

It can't be. The Iris Torien had come to know and love was genuine and free with her emotions. She would not have kept something so important a secret. She would never have toyed with Torien's heart so...thoughtlessly.

"Don't look so devastated, Pacias. These flighty models are like that."

Torien didn't respond. Couldn't.

"If it's any consolation, she was supposed to leave for Paris three weeks ago, but she extended her vacation. I assume that was to spend a little more time with you."

It wasn't any consolation.

"Let me make it easier for you." Moreno reached inside her jacket and extracted an envelope from the inner breast pocket. She held it out.

Torien's gaze froze on the offering then slowly lifted to her boss's face. "What is this?"

Moreno twisted her mouth to one side. "We'll keep things clean. Consider it a bonus for doing such great work with the gardens. It's enough for you and your sister to take a couple weeks off and visit your family. By then, Iris will be in Paris where she belongs, and you, my dear, will actually have a job to return to."

The words left unsaid spoke volumes compared to those actually voiced. Torien swallowed thickly, recognizing the "bonus" for what it was. Torien's entire body tensed. What kind of woman did Moreno think she was? "And if I don't take it?"

"Then I'm afraid I will have to let you go." Moreno's eyes telegraphed ruthlessness. "You did, after all, ignore my number one house rule."

A long moment stretched between them, Torien's eyes on the envelope, Moreno's eyes on Torien. The old Torien might have taken the money simply to keep from placing her family in a difficult financial position, but this time…she could not. If she'd learned anything from her loving family, from Iris, from a wellspring of strength deep inside herself, it was that people who loved each other stuck together.

Through the good times.

The bad.

Through the everything and the nothing.

No. Torien wouldn't gamble away Iris's love like a ten-dollar poker chip, even if this all-encompassing love had been one-sided, as *la patrona* claimed.

She stood. "Keep your money, *Señora* Moreno. If Iris wishes to leave for Paris, she can do so on her own."

The envelope crunched as Moreno's fist tightened. "You're making a massive mistake, Pacias." She stepped closer, but Torien still had a good eight inches of height on her and used it to her advantage. "If you stand in the way of Iris's business deal, I'll make sure you never work a decent job in this town again."

"You misunderstand. I'm not standing in the way of anything. I simply decline your…offer." Pride straightened Torien's shoulders. She peered down her nose at Moreno. "Iris is so much more than a business deal, Geraline. More than dollar signs and fame. It is a shame you cannot see that." She paused. "You want me to leave?" Torien hiked one shoulder as if it didn't matter a bit. "Then I will leave. But not because you paid me off. I will leave...because I love her."

CHAPTER TEN

The wipers beat a steady rhythm against the windshield of Madeira's truck. Iris stared straight ahead, her eyes alternately blurring and focusing on the diagonal shoots of rain caught in the white beams of the headlights. Madeira had been chauffeuring her around aimlessly for an hour. They had driven by the Círculo de Esperanza house several times, but Torien's white truck wasn't there. Iris hated the thoughts in her head, but she needed to exorcise the demons. "Would she be...with another woman?"

"Absolutely not, Iris." A vein in Madeira's temple pumped. "I know my sister. She wouldn't do that to you."

Madeira had been so patient with Iris's quickfire questions. Iris supposed she should let the poor thing off the hook. Stirring in her seat, she reached over and squeezed Madeira's forearm. "Look, we aren't going to figure this out tonight. Stop somewhere. Let me fill your gas tank, then you can take me to Geraline's."

"Don't be ridiculous. I'm as upset as you are. I've never seen my sister like this."

Iris bit her lip to stop her quivering chin, fearing it would rev her crying engine into the red zone. Everything had been on track with her and Torien, and only getting better. They had met in the gazebo as planned, Iris's heart filled with anticipation for a wonderful night together. Instead, in the short time it had taken

Iris to shower and change, Torien had transformed from smiling and flirtatious to painfully polite.

Distant.

Brooding, even.

"God, what happened?" she whispered, for the millionth time, it seemed.

"*Yo no sé.* She looked distracted when the two of you arrived at the bar, but she's been working hard." Madeira shrugged. "I thought it was that. Did you tell her about Paris?"

A beat passed, during which a sword of guilt impaled her. Iris hadn't wanted to spook Tori, but instead she had lied to her. A lie of omission was no better than an outright lie, and to an honorable woman like Torien, it could only spell disaster. "No."

"Ah, Iris." Madeira's sigh filled the space. "Could she have found out?" She came to a stop at a red light, and their eyes met in the darkness of the truck cab.

She remembered Antoine and Geraline, dread screeching in her ears. "Yes. Fuck. Yes, she could have found out." Urgency rattled her composure, trembled in her hands. "Take me to Geraline's, Madi. I'm going to learn the truth from the source."

Iris shoved through the ornate front door, and the only thing that prevented her from yelling for Antoine and Geraline at the top of her lungs was respect for any of the household help who might still be around. She stomped through the living room, out onto the stone terrace, into the screening room—nothing. As her frustration level mounted, muffled voices floated toward her from the kitchen.

Fueled, she stalked that way, ready to bring down the wrath of God if either of them had anything to do with Torien's torment, her sudden desertion. For a moment, Iris stood stock still in the doorway to the massive kitchen and stared. Antoine and Geraline sat at the chrome table, feet hooked on the chair rungs and elbows propped before them. The single chrome fixture above the table lit their faces but cast the rest of the room in shadows. A bit of light gleamed dully off the polished steel Sub-Zero fridge.

"Darling." Geraline stood, kissing one of Iris's cheeks, then the other. "So good to see you made it back."

"What did you say to her?"

Geraline exchanged an innocent glance with Antoine. "To whom, cupcake?"

"Screw you, Gerri. Screw all your placating bullshit." Iris's hands were shaking, and she clenched her fists to stop the telltale motion. "You know damn well who. Torien. What did you tell her?"

"You mean about Paris?" Geraline asked, her tone infuriatingly blasé. "Simply what you should've told her weeks ago. That you were leaving. In a week." She shrugged. "It's the truth, so I assumed she already knew. I'm so sorry if I ruined your fun—"

"Save it." Iris paced a few feet away, fearing she would punch Geraline if she stood too close. She spun back, anger pounding icy in her ears. "You knew exactly what you intended to achieve when you dropped your little bomb on Torien. How could you? How dare you toy with my life like this?"

Geraline scoffed and took her seat again. "Cupcake, calm down. She's the gardener. Granted, she's eye candy, which is why I hired her in the first place, but—"

"Who in the hell do you think you are?" Iris gasped.

Gerri tossed her silver hair and sighed, as though it took everything within her to suffer through another model tantrum. "I *think* I'm your business manager, Iris, watching out for your welfare like I have always done."

"My business welfare, Geraline. *Business.* You don't own me. No one ever asked you, nor are you paid, to advise me on my personal life."

Geraline pursed her lips and stared at her hands folded in front of her on the table. "If you must know, I'm a little disappointed in

Ms. Pacias. I specifically told her to keep away from the guests, and yet she seems to have done"—cold eyes lifted to Iris's— "quite the opposite. You know how I feel about that."

Iris struggled to school her voice. "For your information, I sought Torien out, not vice versa. She has been a good friend to me."

"And yet…you neglected to tell her about Paris." Geraline cringed with fake sympathy, but her eyes glittered with hardness. "Those one-sided friendships always end badly, dear."

The statement might as well have been a slap to her face. About this one thing, Geraline was right. *Torien* had been a good friend. Iris had not. She sighed. "Tori didn't do anything wrong. Have you seen your precious gardens? They're gorgeous. More gorgeous than ever."

"I never said she wasn't good at her job."

"Then don't punish her because of my indiscretions." Her mind reeled and futile rage churned in her stomach.

Geraline's face remained imperturbable, and all at once Iris realized this entire conversation was useless. Gerri would never understand how Iris could fall in love with an average woman, a pure loving soul. Never. If Iris wanted her life to change, she needed to take the first step. "I'm not going to Paris," she said distractedly, almost as if the words surprised her.

Geraline barked out one loud, short laugh. "Oh. Yes, you are, Iris. You're just upset now, and—"

"No!" Iris yelled.

Gerri's mouth snapped shut.

Iris shook her head. "Listen to me closely, Ger. *Look* at me." She waited until she had her business manager's absolute, undivided attention. "I quit." She snapped her hands out flat. "I'm out of the game. Cancel the contract however you have to, but I'm not going. France isn't a good fit for me anymore. Maybe it never was."

For the first time, Geraline's confidence seemed to falter. Her face blanched, leaving rounds of blush standing out garishly on her cheeks. "Iris, be reasonable. This is a multi-million-dollar—"

"I don't give a shit about the money! I don't need any more money, can't you see that?" She moved closer. "I have more money than I'll need in this lifetime, and yet I've been unhappy for so long. I...don't want to go. I *won't* go."

"You're giving up that great assignment for some chick with dirt under her nails?" Antoine scoffed, incredulous.

She pointed toward Antoine without looking at him. "Get his stupid ass out of here, Geraline. I mean it. Or this discussion is over."

After searching her face for several moments, Geraline swallowed. "Antoine, give us some privacy."

When Antoine had slouched from the room, she took a seat across from her longtime manager.

Geraline clasped both of Iris's hands in her own. "Listen, you are basing a major decision on the wrong thing. A woman? My *gardener*?"

"This has nothing to do with Torien. It's me. Meeting her might have given me the impetus, but...I've changed." All of a sudden, having taken the difficult step, she felt weary. She hung her head and closed her eyes. There was only one place she wanted to be if she couldn't be with Torien: in the gardens, surrounded by all the beautiful things they'd created together. "Cancel the contract. I don't care what you have to do."

"If you have some romantic notion of running off with Pacias, you might want to rethink it." A pointed pause ensued. "I've already spoken with her."

Iris's gaze shot up, and dread pulsed through her veins, slow and oily. "W-what did you tell her?"

Geraline shrugged. "I didn't have to tell her much after dropping the news about Paris. You might as well have paid the woman for her services, Iris, for how she felt. It showed all over her face."

A small gasp of agony escaped her lips.

"But just for insurance"—Geraline's eyes swept up to meet Iris's—"I made her a small offer."

"Offer?" Nausea roiled in Iris's stomach.

"You know, a few thousand bucks to make herself scarce until you came to your senses and went on with your career. That way...she could keep her job, take care of her family. Otherwise—" Geraline made a regretful face.

"You fucking bribed her?" Iris rasped. Her extremities went dead cold and her lips trembled. This couldn't be happening. "You're lying." Her head started to shake in denial, and she couldn't stop it. "Torien would never sell her soul for a job."

"Iris, honey, she didn't sell her soul. She sold *yours*." Geraline leaned forward and lowered her tone to a whisper. "Pacias took the money."

"I don't believe you." Blood slammed through Iris's brain. Her eyes strayed to the kitchen window beyond which lay the night-darkened gardens.

"Suit yourself, but go check the gardener's cottage. I just hope when you realize she's gone, you'll come to your senses." Geraline extracted two airline tickets from the inner pocket of her jacket. "I've booked us on a flight to Paris. We can leave on the red-eye."

The moment stilled. "You just don't get it. All I have ever been to you is a commodity." Her words didn't even shake anymore. Rage had smoothed them to a diamond hardness she wished she had cultivated long ago in her career. "Not anymore. I don't care if Torien is out there or not. I don't care if she took your money. In fact, I hope she did. But none of that changes anything." Iris extracted her hands from Geraline's. "I am not going to Paris. Ever."

❖

Torien is gone.

She was gone, and Geraline said she'd taken the bribe money.

Grief and astonishment cut through Iris. It had to be a mistake. And even if it wasn't, even if Torien had taken the money…Iris knew there would be a damn good reason. She needed to see Tori, to talk this out. But she couldn't bear to leave the garden just yet, their special place. Her eyes strayed from the gazebo steps where they first met, to the front porch of the *cabaña* where they'd first kissed, to the spigot where she'd first seen Torien's half-naked body.

So many precious firsts.

She wandered through the gardens until she came upon the bed of irises she and Torien had planted too late in the season. Tori had given them a chance, nurtured them as best she could, and with any luck, they'd survive.

A woman like that wouldn't…just walk away.

Distraught and distracted, Iris somehow managed to throw her belongings into a leather duffel and call a cab to meet her down the block from Geraline's. She eventually made it to Torien's house in Círculo de Esperanza. The taxi swished away on the rain-soaked street, and Iris found herself just standing there. Terrified to go to the door and find her gone. Terrified to find her there.

Purely…terrified.

But home at the moment or not, Torien wouldn't be gone.

She wouldn't abandon her sister.

But what about us?

Still hesitant, Iris turned toward the beautiful community garden they had created together. The rain had let up, but the droplets decorated every leaf and petal and branch, reflecting the glow of the hunter's moon like a fistful of carelessly strewn diamonds. Her feet carried her to one of the benches, and she sank onto it with a sigh, threading her fingers into the front of her hair. The neighborhood was so quiet at night, such a different landscape in the darkness.

God…if only she'd had some clue as to Torien's torment when she'd asked, "What are you thinking?" at the bar. Had that been earlier tonight? It seemed like a lifetime ago. The entire garden project seemed a lifetime ago.

Why hadn't she told Torien about Paris?

Shame, like an unfriendly dog, snapped at her body, and she wanted to curl into a ball to fend it off. Everyone she had met on the Rainbow Project had been kind to her, accepting her without question, without conditions. But the first person Torien met from Iris's world had treated her like a mangy stray. Gerri had bribed Tori, disparaged her character, demolished her livelihood. The whole situation was such a colossal disaster, and it was completely Iris's fault. Was it any wonder Torien had turned tail and run?

Headlights swept a golden streak over the garden. The rumble of a familiar truck brought Iris up off that bench as if she'd accidentally sat on a rattlesnake.

Torien? Could it be?

Throat tight with the need to see her, Iris hurried to the small picket fence enclosing the baby garden beds and watched Tori parallel park in front of the house. The interior light came on when she popped the truck door. Their eyes met through the windshield, and both women froze.

Iris stood her ground. She ached with tender emotion just seeing Torien's regal face, though her heart cramped at Tori's ravaged expression. Iris ached to touch her, inhale her scent, make it all better. But this was real life, and some problems couldn't just be kissed away.

Fact: Geraline had told Torien about Paris.

Iris hadn't.

Could this breathtakingly honorable woman ever forgive her?

Torien stepped from the truck, first one boot sole, then the other striking the pavement. The closing door echoed loudly in the quiet night, and in the distance, a dog barked, a chain-link fence rattled. Tori stared over the hood of her truck, eyes sorrowful. "Hi."

"Hi," Iris repeated, on a weak exhale.

They mentally circled, wary as wild animals, neither wanting to make a move—the *wrong* move—too quickly.

"Tori, I've been so worried—" Her throat caught, and she looked away for a moment, but her gaze drifted back to Torien automatically...the proverbial compass needle trained to true North. "I didn't know where you went, what happened. I'm so sorry..."

"I am sorry, too. For leaving you at the bar like that," Tori said, her voice husky with pain. She ran a hand slowly down her face. So many things left unsaid. The important things.

Iris shook her head, the motion too jerky, wrought with fear. "No. That doesn't matter. I'm...Tori, *I'm* sorry I didn't tell you about Paris before you found out."

There it was.

The ugly lie erected between them like a thick glass wall.

Iris watched Tori's throat move, a deep, slow swallow.

"Is it true, then? Are you leaving?" She came around to the front bumper, gaze never straying from Iris's, stopping in front of the license tag. Torien's rain-slicked arms hung limply at her sides, sculpted with sinew and muscle, accented by shadow and moonlight. But her manner remained...tentative.

"No. I'm not leaving."

A beat passed. "What?"

"I'm not going to Paris, Tori."

Confusion pulled Torien's brows together. She shook it away. "But Moreno said—"

"Let me explain," Iris said. "I was supposed to go. For—"

"Three years," Torien said.

Iris eased forward and braced her hand against a telephone pole almost directly across the street from Tori. "Yes. But I am breaking the contract."

"No," Torien rasped, as if someone had kicked her. "Don't do it. You must go or you'll regret it forever."

Startled by the vehemence of Tori's response, Iris stepped back and stumbled on a loose stone. She felt as if she'd shown up for her life one day late. "No. I won't regret anything." She sighed. "I thought you'd be...happy."

"Happy?" Torien repeated, incredulity in her tone.

"Yes, about...us. A chance to—"

"Don't you see, Iris? There *is* no 'us' if you give up yourself for me." Two more steps and Torien stood in the middle of the street, just short of the painted line that separated them. "I cannot stand in the way of your life, *mi ángel*. Don't put me there. I have nothing to offer you. I have"—her voice broke, stripped and hollow—"nothing."

Iris's insides stung raw, and disbelief tingled her extremities. "I never asked you for anything, and—Jesus—you've never stood in the way of anything I wanted. Ever. I pushed my way into your life, and you let me. I shouldn't have done it, but I don't regret it."

Tori's head cocked to the side.

"I don't," Iris said. "You helped me find myself—"

"Bullshit."

The word rang out like a shot, and Iris flinched.

"*This* is not you, Irisíta." Torien gestured angrily around them, her words bleak, forced through the pain. "A run-down neighborhood that everyone and her uncle is trying to escape?"

"I don't want to escape it," Iris said.

Torien laughed, but the sound held no humor. "Be realistic. This is my world. As good as it gets. You belong in the limelight, not here."

Iris moved around the pole, leaning her rigid back against it.

"I don't want the limelight," she said, calm conviction in every single word. "I haven't wanted that for a long time, Tori. You know that about me. You know *me*."

Torien looked away, anguish in the set of her jaw.

"I just…didn't know what I wanted," Iris ventured. "Until I met you."

"No, damnit. I cannot bear the responsibility for ruining your career."

Iris shook her head, just as the rain started up again. In the distance, ominous thunder rolled. "Tori, the timing looks bad, but I didn't make this decision only because of you. I have been unhappy with my career for a long time. But it's all I've ever known." She paused, schooled her words. "Being around you, around *this neighborhood*, the volunteers on the project—all of that made me realize exactly why I've been so unsettled." She leveled Tori with a gaze, the rain kicking a steamy fog up around their legs. "I came to apologize to you, Tori. But I'm not going to Paris. Whether you want me or not, even if you never want to see me again…I told Geraline to cancel the contract. And I meant it."

A long, worried sigh escaped Torien's lips. "Ah, baby girl, you don't know what you've done. To give up your life for another person…it will destroy you."

"I'm not giving up my life. I'm finally going to live my life." This close, she could see turmoil raging just beneath Torien's surface. Not more than twelve feet of space separated them, but it felt like an ocean. A whole world. *We live in different worlds*, Torien had said. And she'd been right. Would they ever be able to reach across this distance, this bridgeless space between Iris's reality and Torien's? Did Torien even want to?

"I'm not going to Paris," Iris said again, firmly, shoving strands of wet hair away from her face. "I'm sorry I didn't tell you. And I'm…sorrier than you'll ever know that I caused you problems with your job."

"You don't owe me any explanations."

"Yes, I do." Iris licked raindrops from her lips. "Geraline told me. What she did. Offering you money."

Dark, angry eyes jerked to Iris's face, and in that moment, she absolutely knew Torien hadn't taken Geraline's bribe. "Ah, the money." A brittle pause. "And you thought I took it?"

Her brief hesitation was a mistake; it showed in Torien's crushed expression. "Gerri told me you did, but I never believed it. But I wouldn't have blamed you if you had."

"I didn't."

"I don't care, Tori. You should have. Fuck Geraline."

"Hijole madre." Torien shook her head and stared at her feet for a long time. When she met Iris's gaze again, her features were etched with pain. "We have to talk, *mi ángel.*"

"I understand," Iris said, her tone solemn. She noted the agonized breathing in the rise and fall of Torien's chest.

"No. You…don't understand. I need to tell you…what I did," Torien said, her voice hoarse, halting.

Something bad. Iris could see it in her stormy eyes.

But she hadn't taken the money.

What…?

"We don't have to talk about this," Iris whispered, not wanting to hear anything that would crush their precarious connection. Not wanting to lose Torien—again—before she ever truly had her. The rain pelted them harder, and she raised her voice over the sound of it splattering on the pavement. "There's always time for talk later."

"Now. I must." Anguish eclipsed Torien's features. "You need to know the kind of woman I am before you turn your back on…your whole world."

"I do know you, honey. I *do.*"

"No," came Torien's vehement denial. "No one knows."

Iris's fingers tingled, terrified of what Torien might confess. And yet, she wanted nothing more than to be there for her, to listen to her. Whatever Torien's secret, surely Iris's deception was worse. She shivered in the cold rain. "Tell me."

Torien peered up at the blackness, dark lashes blinking against the downpour. The skies cried for them, drenching them both. "Come inside, Iris. This is ridiculous, our meetings in the rain. Your teeth are chattering, for God's sake."

Iris nodded, then shouldered her duffel bag and crossed the last few feet toward Torien. Without asking, Torien took the bag from Iris, and together they walked silently up the path. She should've felt good to have been invited into Torien's home, but she didn't. Not yet. Nothing was settled between them, and the fear kept her teetered off balance.

Torien stepped aside to let Iris enter first, then followed her in. Iris traversed the room, her arms wrapped around her torso, chilled to the marrow. When she heard the deadbolt sliding into place, she turned back. Torien stood there on the doormat, eyes remote and ravaged. Every few seconds, rivulets of water would reach the end of her chin or her fingers and drip off onto the floor. Trails of water drained down her back. If Torien's jeans felt anything like Iris's—as if they were made of lead and lined with sandpaper—neither of them was too comfortable. It didn't matter. She glanced around the room. "Who else is h-here?"

"It's just us."

She nodded, infuriatingly unable to control the shivers. "S-so, t-talk to me."

"You need dry clothes first."

"Tori, I'm f-fine."

"Then humor me." She arched an eyebrow, then left the room and returned with a flannel robe for Iris, a towel for herself. She lifted her chin toward the hallway. "You can change in the restroom." At Iris's hesitation, she added, "I'm not going anywhere. I'll be right here."

A few minutes later, wrapped tightly in the robe that held Torien's alluring scent, Iris returned to the living room. She hadn't expected to feel self-conscious, vulnerable—but she did. Tori had dried off and slipped into jeans with wear-holes in various places and a dry, faded T-shirt. Her feet were bare, which struck Iris as achingly intimate and poignantly sexy. She recalled that day in the garden, catching Torien with her shirt off in the potting shed. *Where it all started...* Torien glanced up, and Iris cleared her throat. "Hello, again," she said, wistfully. Remembering... always remembering. "I'm surprised to see you here."

Torien's still troubled eyes keyed on the cue immediately, warming slightly. "I'm staying here, remember?"

Enough play. Iris claimed a chair across from where Tori stood with her shoulder propped on the door jamb. "I'm all ears."

Torien's focus moved inward. Her throat constricted several times, over a memory that was obviously so painful, she could hardly verbalize it. Finally she asked, "Do you recall our conversation about my father?" The words empty, raw, hushed.

The subject one-eighty surprised Iris. She blinked. "Of course I do."

Torien's chest rose and fell with unshed tears. "That I was angry? After he died?"

"Yes."

"The truth is...I did not want to care for my family when it happened. I wanted to live out my big dreams, too." Torien's voice came out laced with shame. She flicked her arm out in disgust. "So, you see? I am no better than him."

"No. No, Tori, that's not true," Iris implored.

"It is. It's my truth."

Jesus. Iris never imagined *this* was the anvil of guilt weighing on Torien's conscience. She'd been mired in her overblown sense of responsibility for so long...this on top of everything else was too much. Iris wanted to cross the room and hold her so badly, her knees trembled. But she sensed Tori's need for distance. "You were a young woman. Young women are supposed to dream."

"Didn't you hear what I said?" Torien's voice raised, but not in anger. She sucked a couple ragged breaths. "I didn't want to support them, Iris. Please listen."

"I am, honey."

"I wanted to walk away from my family and chase my own selfish dreams. What kind of woman am I?"

Iris frowned. "But that's ridiculous."

Torien stiffened, the shock on her face swiftly crumbling into tightly controlled tears. She slid down the wall and buried her face in her hands.

The show of emotion seemed so uncharacteristic, it caught Iris off guard. Regaining her composure, she stood. "It doesn't matter what you felt. You *didn't* walk away." She closed the distance between them in two long strides, knelt, and enveloped Tori—strong, steadfast, sorrowful Tori—in her arms. She pressed her forehead against Torien's knuckles and simply let her silently mourn. "You faced your responsibilities like a woman when you weren't much more than a teenager. For God's sake, you have nothing to be ashamed of."

"I do." She sniffed, smacked away the tears. "I resented him, Iris. Resented the hell out of his burden being thrown in my lap. And yet, I am *just like him*." Her eyes sought understanding, lashes spiky and dark with tears.

"I'm not...sure what you mean."

"Don't give up your life for me, *mi ángel*. God help me, I am my father's daughter. *De tal padre, tal hija*."

"It's not true," Iris said, emphatically. "You didn't walk away—"

"It doesn't matter." Torien extracted herself from Iris's embrace and backed away. "You believe me to be someone I'm not."

Iris wrapped her hands around Torien's wrists, not wholly certain of the connection. "How's that?"

"I am still chasing foolish dreams, just like *Papá*," she

rasped. "I could have taken Moreno's blood money and kept my easy job, kept helping my mother and sisters…but I didn't. I didn't take the money. And now I have nothing and they will all suffer."

"I'm…so sorry."

Torien flicked the apology away. "I'm not looking for an apology. I'm just…trying to explain. Despite my responsibilities, I couldn't"—her voice cracked—"I couldn't bear to cheapen what we have, Iris. Not even for my family's security." She pounded her fists on her thighs. "You are the big dream I am chasing now, and again I've disappointed my family like *Papá* did. Except this time, it's on me."

"Tori, I will never come between you and your fam—"

"Irisíta." Torien folded her into an almost desperate embrace, holding her so tightly, Iris couldn't pull a full breath. "Jesus, babe, I don't deserve you. Deserve this." Her strong, work-worn hands stroked the sides of Iris's arms gently. "And yet, I don't want to walk away again."

Iris wrapped her arms around Torien's trim waist. "I don't want you to."

"Go to Paris."

"No."

"Please, Iris. I don't want to be the cause of—"

"Shh. Listen to me. Your life is not like his. Geraline isn't giving you a choice in the matter. Don't sell your soul for her." Iris kissed Torien's damp eyelids, her nose, her tear-streaked cheek. "I've done that for far too long, sold my soul for what Geraline wanted, for what the modeling industry wanted. *That's* why I'm not going to Paris, Tori. It's not my dream." She looked deeply in Torien's eyes. "Not anymore."

A small spark of hesitant hope caught fire in Torien's expression, and Iris fanned the flames. "If we don't fit in either of the worlds we've known, we'll create a new one. Our world, Tori. Yours and mine. That's my new dream. You're my future."

"Ah, *mi ángel*…" Torien reached for Iris, and she fell willingly into Tori's arms, their mouths meeting with an inevitable passion. Through their kisses, Iris found her courage. Reaching between them, she untied the robe and let it slip from her shoulders until she stood in the safety of Tori's arms naked—literally and emotionally. Her rite of passage from a life she hated to one filled with hope.

"Jesus…so beautiful." Torien groaned, smoothing those palms over Iris's skin, kissing, kissing, kissing her lips, forehead, neck, and back to her lips.

Breathless, Iris pulled her head back and regarded Tori through love-drunk eyes. She slid her hands under Torien's T-shirt and up her body to cup her small, firm breasts.

Torien inhaled sharply, arched into Iris's palms.

"Say yes, Tori." She swirled her fingertips around Torien's hard nipples. "Believe in it. In us. Tell me you do."

Tori furrowed her fingers into Iris's wet hair and studied her for a moment, then planted several light kisses on her lips, the corners of her mouth, her throat, her bare shoulders. "Yes," she murmured, sliding her hands down Iris's back to cup her shapely curved ass. She pulled Iris into her, thrust her hips into soft… wet…heat. "I believe in us, Irisíta."

Passion surged through Iris's veins, and she knew the only thing real in her life was this woman. This moment. "Love me."

"I do."

"No. I mean…*love* me, like I'm going to love you."

Torien's mouth came to Iris's with a matching fervor, and they lost themselves in the safety of each other. Torien stilled, breathing jagged, the motions of her body speaking volumes of wordless communication. "I…have to—"

"I know."

Torien pulled Iris onto one of her thighs, clasping her hips and increasing the pressure. Sweet tension boiled exactly where Iris wanted it most. "I need—"

"Me, too, Tori." Their gazes tangled for just a moment before, in a fury of action, Iris found herself swept into Torien's arms, down the hall, into a modestly decorated bedroom. She became aware of sensations in increments, cataloging them in her mind's eye like snapshots.

More firsts.

She never wanted to forget…

The gentle give of the mattress against her back.

Moonlight slanting silvery through the window.

Torien kneeling between her thighs, pulling that T-shirt over her head as Iris reached for her button fly.

It could've been a nanosecond, it could've been a lifetime, but Iris sighed when Torien's warm body covered hers, closing out everything but the beauty of skin on hot skin, Torien's trembling breaths, her desire so stark and tender and real.

"Touch me."

"Ah, Iris…" Tori whispered. She caressed Iris's body like no other woman ever had—as if Tori were starved for her but fearful of consuming her whole. Iris's senses filled with Tori, the sight and scents and warmth of her.

Hitched breaths.

The hot warm places tightening…opening…throbbing.

The dizzying pull of Tori's mouth on her nipples.

Iris moaned, lifting her hips to press closer. She wanted Tori on her, in her, around her until she couldn't inhale without Tori having to exhale. She had known Torien wouldn't be a tentative lover, but her intense focus and passion was like a drug, and Iris? Hooked.

Tori raised up on one elbow, reaching her other arm behind Iris to pull her tighter into the rocking motion of their bodies connecting. "Tell me what you want."

Iris smiled. "I don't have to tell you, sweet. You already know."

Tori slid one hand between the pressure of her insistent thigh and Iris's slickness, rocking, rocking. Her touch was a promise, her gaze a caress. "Inside?"

Enough talking. Iris reached for that tantalizing wrist and pushed Torien's fingers deep inside her own body. "Yeah…" she sighed. "Right there." She kissed the gasp from Tori's mouth, then started to move, undulate. Hot and throbbing, Iris raised up to take more of Torien inside her. She opened herself to Torien, their gazes, bodies, hearts connected.

Torien pushed into Iris's warmth. "Like that?"

"Harder. I'm not going to break."

Torien sucked a breath in through her teeth, resting her forehead on Iris's breasts and closing her eyes, allowing her body to take over and give Iris exactly what she craved. The room filled with the erotic scent of their bodies, the whispers, sighs, and moans from their lips and hearts. Torien needed to be so deep inside Iris, they would never be separated again. She wanted to hear her name in Iris's sighs, feel the quiver of her legs and know that they'd connected so intimately, no one could ever breach the safety of their love.

Iris's breath quickened; her back arched. Torien could feel the impending orgasm gripping her fingers, but didn't want it to end. Not yet. Sliding out of Iris's warmth, despite the moan of protest, Torien nibbled her way down Iris's body until her mouth captured that warm aching center. Iris's body bucked, and she cried out.

Torien lifted her head. "I want to take you there, Irisíta, with my tongue."

She watched Iris's abdomen contract. "Yes," she hissed.

Reaching her hand up, she slipped a moist finger into Iris's mouth at the same time she claimed Iris again with her tongue, gently with her teeth. The sensation of Iris sucking her finger fired her desire, and she pulled and swirled that most womanly part of Iris until her rapid breathing and shaking thighs told Torien…this was the spot.

Iris gripped her wrist and arched up, her entire body tensing as she moaned and cried out and came in a rush of heat against Torien's tongue.

Torien managed to smile, never breaking stride. She wanted all of Iris. Now. Not just her body—all of her. Just as Torien thought Iris had melted into a boneless aftermath, she found herself flipped deftly onto her back.

Torien blinked up at the woman she loved.

Iris reached between their bodies, her eyes fluttering shut when she touched Torien's hot, wet need.

"This isn't over," Tori said, "is it?"

A smile lit on Iris's face. "Tori...*mi adora para siempre*—my forever love," Iris murmured, sliding easily into Tori's body, "not even close."

Much later, as Iris and Torien lay tangled in each other and near sleep, Iris whispered, "I love you, Tori."

Torien shifted, pulling Iris closer. *"Te quiero, mi Irisíta."* She kissed the back of her neck, sending a wash of shivers down Iris's spine. "You know...I *would* give up the world for you."

"I know. As I would for you. But guess what?"

"Mmm?" Torien asked.

"Neither of us has to give up anything for each other. We simply have to...be. It's our world now, Tori. And no one can touch us here."

"It's like a dream."

"But real."

"It's us."

Iris sighed. "Yeah. It is. And it couldn't be more perfect."

Epilogue

The sunshine hit the large Victorian house in such a way that Iris thought she had never before seen anything so beautiful. It had been hard work converting it into a workable center of operations, but they had pulled it off, and today they would present themselves to the world. News vans crowded the streets and throngs of people had begun gathering around the front yard, which was closed off with a fat red ribbon.

Torien approached her, looking ill at ease in her new suit, but her face softened when their eyes met. She touched Iris's cheek. "You almost ready, *mi ángel?*"

"I have never been more ready."

"*Te quiero,* Irisíta. More than I ever thought possible."

"Didn't I tell you everything would work out if we stuck together?" Iris kissed Tori, long and slow and private.

"I should listen to you more often."

Iris laughed. "Can I get that on tape?"

Hand in hand they approached the house. Cameras flashed like lightning bugs, capturing the house, the newly erected sign, their glowing faces. Under the watchful eyes of television cameras, they placed the oversized scissors in cutting position over the ribbon, and hesitated. Torien's eyes went to the large sign, and Iris followed her gaze. Her heart constricted.

OUR WORLD: Growing Communities One Plant at a Time

was the most important and ambitious project the Iris Lujan Foundation had ever undertaken. And the one closest to their hearts. They had hatched the idea for the partially grant-funded enterprise the day after Iris had turned her back on Paris. They'd spent all day in bed at Torien's Círculo de Esperanza town house, making love and trying to figure out where their unmoored lives would take them. Eventually, they'd docked here.

It had taken more than a year for that initial idea to sprout into a fully bloomed concept. But they had done it. OUR WORLD's mission was to mentor volunteer groups all over the country, teaching them to bring community gardens to economically disadvantaged areas. With Iris as their spokesperson, they had already raised millions of dollars, and Torien at the helm inspired people to work hard and reach for their goals.

"Ms. Lujan!" someone hollered.

The media was waiting. Iris and Torien looked directly into each other's eyes, and after a quick kiss, she whispered, "Ready?"

"*Sí.* Always ready for you."

Their eyes never left each other's faces as they closed the oversized scissors. One slice and the ribbon fell away. Around them, cheers filled the sunny block. Toasts and applause and glee-filled embraces. Tears stung Iris's eyes as she wrapped Torien in her arms, rained kisses on her face. Soon Madeira had joined the hug, followed by their mother and the twins, Paloma, and Emie and her partner, Gia. Volunteers from the Rainbow Project surged forward, showering them with honeysuckle blossoms, whooping and hollering.

Reporters began lobbing questions, but they were both too choked with emotion to answer.

"Where is the first garden going to be?"

"How many volunteers do you have on board so far?"

"Iris! Torien! One quick question, please." They turned, and the reporter held out a small tape recorder, a wide grin on her face. "From world-class model to philanthropist. The world wants to know. How'd this idea come about?"

Iris lost herself in Torien's eyes, knowing she had never been so happy in all her life.

"Tell them, *mi ángel*," Torien encouraged.

Iris kissed her, unmindful of the flashbulbs and footage, only knowing this was their moment, their world.

She turned to the reporter, who had flushed bright red from their infectious passion.

"How'd this come about?" Iris repeated, raising her voice so the murmur would cease. When it did, she wound her fingers with Torien's and squeezed. "Let's just say it all started with one big dream."

About the Author

Lea Santos has been concocting tall tales since she was a child, according to her mother. Usually these had to do with where she was, who she was with, and whether or not she'd finished her math homework (which she hadn't). When it came time to pick a career, Lea waffled, then dabbled in everything from guiding tours in Europe, to police work, to bookkeeping for an exotic bird and reptile company—probably not the best choice, since (1) she never did finish that math, and (2) the Komodo dragons freaked her out. (A lot.) She eventually decided to go with her strengths and continue spinning wild stories, except this time, she'd turn them into whole books and call it a career. She rarely lies anymore about where she's been or who she was with...

Books Available From Bold Strokes Books

The Devil be Damned by Ali Vali. The fourth book in the best-selling Cain Casey Devil series. (978-1-60282-159-0)

Descent by Julie Cannon. Shannon Roberts and Caroline Davis compete in the world of world-class bike racing and pretend that the fire between them is just professional rivalry, not desire. (978-1-60282-160-6)

Kiss of Noir by Clara Nipper. Nora Delany is a hard-living, sweet-talking woman who can't say no to a beautiful babe or a friend in danger—a darkly humorous homage to a bygone era of tough broads and murder in steamy New Orleans. (978-1-60282-161-3)

Under Her Skin by Lea Santos. Supermodel Lilly Lujan hasn't a care in the world, except life is lonely in the spotlight—until Mexican gardener Torien Pacias sees through Lilly's facade and offers gentle understanding and friendship when Lilly most needs it. (978-1-60282-162-0)

Fierce Overture by Gun Brooke. Helena Forsythe is a hard-hitting CEO who gets what she wants by taking no prisoners when negotiating—until she meets a woman who convinces her that charm may be the way to win a battle, and a heart. (978-1-60282-156-9)

Trauma Alert by Radclyffe. Dr. Ali Torveau has no trouble saying no to romance until the day firefighter Beau Cross shows up in her ER and sets her carefully ordered world aflame. (978-1-60282-157-6)

Wolfsbane Winter by Jane Fletcher. Iron Wolf mercenary Deryn faces down demon magic and otherworldly foes with a smile, but she's defenseless when healer Alana wages war on her heart. (978-1-60282-158-3)

Little White Lie by Lea Santos. Emie Jaramillo knows relationships are for other people, and beautiful women like Gia Mendez don't belong anywhere near her boring world of academia—until Gia sets out to convince Emie she has not only brains, but beauty...and that she's the only woman Gia wants in her life. (978-1-60282-163-7)

Witch Wolf by Winter Pennington. In a world where vampires have charmed their way into modern society, where werewolves walk the streets with their beasts disguised by human skin, Investigator Kassandra Lyall has a secret of her own to protect. She's one of them. (978-1-60282-177-4)

Do Not Disturb by Carsen Taite. Ainsley Faraday, a high-powered executive, and rock music celebrity Greer Davis couldn't be less well suited for one another, and yet they soon discover passion has a way of designing its own future. (978-1-60282-153-8)

From This Moment On by PJ Trebelhorn. Devon Conway and Katherine Hunter both lost love and neither believes they will ever find it again—until the moment they meet and everything changes. (978-1-60282-154-5)

Vapor by Larkin Rose. When erotic romance writer Ashley Vaughn decides to take her research into the bedroom for a night of passion with Victoria Hadley, she discovers that fact is hotter than fiction. (978-1-60282-155-2)

Wind and Bones by Kristin Marra. Jill O'Hara, award-winning journalist, just wants to settle her deceased father's affairs and leave Prairie View, Montana, far, far behind—but an old girlfriend, a sexy sheriff, and a dangerous secret keep her down on the ranch. (978-1-60282-150-7)

Nightshade by Shea Godfrey. The story of a princess, betrothed as a political pawn, who falls for her intended husband's soldier sister, is a modern-day fairy tale to capture the heart. (978-1-60282-151-4)

Vieux Carré Voodoo by Greg Herren. Popular New Orleans detective Scotty Bradley just can't stay out of trouble—especially when an old flame turns up asking for help. (978-1-60282-152-1)

The Pleasure Set by Lisa Girolami. Laney DeGraff, a successful president of a family-owned bank on Rodeo Drive, finds her comfortable life taking a turn toward danger when Theresa Aguilar, a sleek, sexy lawyer, invites her to join an exclusive, secret group of powerful, alluring women. (978-1-60282-144-6)

A Perfect Match by Erin Dutton. The exciting world of pro golf forms the backdrop for a fast-paced, sexy romance. (978-1-60282-145-3)

Father Knows Best by Lynda Sandoval. High school juniors and best friends Lila Moreno, Meryl Morganstern, and Caressa Thibodoux plan to make the most of the summer before senior year. What they discover that amazing summer about girl power, growing up, and trusting friends and family more than prepares them to tackle that all-important senior year! (978-1-60282-147-7)

The Midnight Hunt by L.L. Raand. Medic Drake McKennan takes a chance and loses, and her life will never be the same—because when she wakes up after surviving a life-threatening illness, she is no longer human. (978-1-60282-140-8)

Long Shot by D. Jackson Leigh. Love isn't safe, which is exactly why equine veterinarian Tory Greyson wants no part of it—until Leah Montgomery and a horse that won't give up convince her otherwise. (978-1-60282-141-5)

In Medias Res by Yolanda Wallace. Sydney has forgotten her entire life, and the one woman who holds the key to her memory, and her heart, doesn't want to be found. (978-1-60282-142-2)

Awakening to Sunlight by Lindsey Stone. Neither Judith or Lizzy is looking for companionship, and certainly not love—but when their lives become entangled, they discover both. (978-1-60282-143-9)

Fever by VK Powell. Hired gun Zakaria Chambers is hired to provide a simple escort service to philanthropist Sara Ambrosini, but nothing is as simple as it seems, especially love. (978-1-60282-135-4)

Truths by Rebecca S. Buck. Two women separated by two hundred years are connected by fate and love. (978-1-60282-146-0)

High Risk by JLee Meyer. Can actress Kate Hoffman really risk all she's worked for to take a chance on love? Or is it already too late? (978-1-60282-136-1)

Spanking New by Clifford Henderson. A poignant, hilarious, unforgettable look at life, love, gender, and the essence of what makes us who we are. (978-1-60282-138-5)

Missing Lynx by Kim Baldwin and Xenia Alexiou. On the trail of a notorious serial killer, Elite Operative Lynx's growing attraction to a mysterious mercenary could be her path to love—or to death. (978-1-60282-137-8)

Magic of the Heart by C.J. Harte. CEO Susan Hettinger and wild, impulsive rock star M.J. Carson couldn't be more different if they tried—but opposites attract in ways neither woman can resist. (978-1-60282-131-6)

Ambereye by Gill McKnight. Jolie Garoul is falling in love with her assistant. The big problem is, Jolie is a werewolf. (978-1-60282-132-3)

Collision Course by C.P. Rowlands. Tragedy leaves Brie O'Malley and Jordan Carter fearful and alone. Can they find the courage to take a second chance on love? (978-1-60282-133-0)

Mephisto Aria by Justine Saracen. Opera singer Katherina Marov's destiny may be to repeat the mistakes of her father when she becomes involved in a dangerous love affair. (978-1-60282-134-7)